A DARING
RETURN

Other books in this series:

A Clever Disguise
A Brilliant Deception

Other books by Kathleen Fuller:

Santa Fe Sunrise
Special Assignment
San Antonio Sunset
San Francisco Serenade

A DARING
RETURN

•

Kathleen Fuller

AVALON BOOKS
NEW YORK

Published by Thomas Bouregy & Co., Inc.
160 Madison Avenue, New York, NY 10016

Library of Congress Cataloging-in-Publication Data

Fuller, Kathleen.
    A daring return / Kathleen Fuller.
        p. cm.
    ISBN 978-0-8034-9967-6
    I. Title.

PS3606.U553D37   2009
813'.6—dc22
                    2009003692

PRINTED IN THE UNITED STATES OF AMERICA
ON ACID-FREE PAPER
BY HADDON CRAFTSMEN, BLOOMSBURG, PENNSYLVANIA

To Tamela Hancock Murray:
for always being there.

Prologue

April 1812

A knot of pain formed in Gavin Parringer's belly as agony enveloped his soul. Standing outside his best friend's house, he struggled with the emotional battle raging inside him. Lights glowed from every room of the house, illuminating the glass windows. The stately manor seemed like a beacon on the darkened London street, and Gavin felt drawn to go inside.

Or rather, to go *back* inside.

He paced the front walk, kicking a stone as he tried to decide what to do. He had already been inside once, an uninvited and unwelcome visitor to the party Colin Dymoke, Baron Chesreton, was hosting. It was the only party Colin had never invited him to, and the only time Gavin had ever crashed one. Yet he had a good reason to break all protocol and attend a party he had no business being at.

Colin's sister, Diana, was the reason.

Never mind that this was *her* engagement party. Or that he was madly in love with her, and she loved someone else. Or that her sister, Emily, had just declared her love for him, and he had to gently but firmly tell her that his heart belonged to only one woman. Or that common sense had finally reigned and he had left the party a few minutes earlier before spoiling the evening for everyone.

He shoved his hand through his hair. Blast, when did everything get so bloody complicated?

But there was one thing that was crystal clear— Diana was making a mistake. A huge mistake. And he had to try and stop her. He wouldn't be able to live with himself if he didn't.

His decision made, Gavin walked back through the doorway and went to the footman standing in the foyer. Gavin knew him from his numerous visits to Colin over the past year, since his friend had married Lily Breckenridge. Striding up to the shorter, rounder man, Gavin said, "I need to write a note."

The footman gave him an odd look, but nodded. "I shall fetch pen and paper for you, my lord," he said, addressing Gavin, a viscount, by his appropriate title. The man then rushed off, leaving Gavin standing in the foyer, hoping not to gain any of the guests' attentions. He quickly returned and gave over the writing materials. Gavin dashed off a few lines, folded the paper haphazardly, and handed it back. "Please give this to Miss Diana at once."

"My lord, she is quite busy entertaining her guests."

"I realize that," Gavin said, trying to keep the impatience out of his voice, "but this is a matter of great import." His gaze narrowed. "Or should I have you fetch Lord Chesreton instead?"

The footman paled, and shook his head. "I shall give this to Miss Diana at once."

Glad the man hadn't called his bluff, Gavin rushed out the house and circled around the back, to the far corner of Colin and Lily's garden, where he had instructed she meet him. As he waited, he prayed his note had conveyed enough urgency to Diana for her not to dismiss his request. After several long, agonizing moments, he saw her come out the back door, looking over her shoulder as if to make sure she hadn't been followed.

When she reached him, he could barely make out her features in the darkened night. But when she turned her face and tilted it upward to look directly at him, a sliver of soft moonlight illuminated her face, effectively stealing the breath from his lungs.

His heart swelled with love for her. She was such a beautiful creature, the loveliest woman in London, not only in his estimation but in almost everyone's opinion as well. Diana Dymoke's beauty was the stuff of legends, and since her debut in London society, she'd had more suitors than any other ingénue in the *ton*. Gavin had counted himself among those suitors, until she had told him she had accepted William Garland's proposal. She had delivered this news rather unceremoniously and with little regard for his feelings, destroying the impression he'd had that he had won her affections and they had a future together. Her revelation had hit him harder than a punch in the gut, breaking his heart into a thousand pieces. He doubted he would ever rebound from her rejection. For him, the only woman in the world was Diana Dymoke, and knowing she would never be his was something he couldn't comprehend.

But his own emotional state was not his reason for wanting to meet with her, and he was thankful she agreed to come out here, even at great personal risk. The spark of anger in her eyes showed that she understood the precariousness of their clandestine meeting. If they were caught together in the dark, alone . . . her reputation would be in ruins, and Gavin would probably be facing pistols at dawn.

"How dare you drag me away from my own engagement party," she hissed, fury coloring her tone. "What is it you want?"

What he wanted was to take her in his arms and never let her go, but he couldn't do that. Instead he had to focus on what he needed to tell her. "You cannot marry William."

She huffed, crossing her arms over the glittery bodice of her gorgeous pale-pink ball gown. "Gavin, I already told you—I do not love you. I love William, and I am going to marry him, and that is the end of this conversation." Spinning around she turned to go, but he snaked out his arm and grasped her shoulder. "Unhand me," she said fiercely, but in a low voice.

He immediately released her, but moved to stand in front of her so he could keep her from leaving. "Diana, listen to me. I am not telling you this out of some misguided attempt to win you back." Although he would if he thought he could. "I am here out of concern for your welfare. You must not marry William. He is a rogue of the worst sort—"

"I will not stand here and listen to you denigrate my future husband, who has been nothing but kind and attentive and loving toward me."

"It is an act, Diana. Trust me, you are not aware of this man's reputation."

"And you are? How? And if he is such a rogue, how come no one else has said anything?"

Gavin paused for a moment, unsure of how much to reveal.

"I am waiting."

He took a deep breath. "I had him investigated."

"You what?" Diana stormed toward him, anger radiating from her perfect body.

With his next breath Gavin inhaled her sweet scent and fought to maintain control. She was even attractive when angry. In fact it gave her a fiery edge he didn't know she possessed. But while he was trying to keep from kissing her, she undoubtedly wanted to clock him over the head. "I did it for you," he said, trying to defend his position. "I had my suspicions about him, so I hired someone to investigate him." He lowered his voice to a whisper. "I am truly sorry to say this to you, but you have to believe me. He will only hurt you."

Anger flashed in her eyes. "The only person hurting me is you. This is a sad little attempt to come between me and the man I love, and I will not tolerate it. Understand me now. You can stop making up lies in hopes of convincing me that we belong together. It will never, ever happen." She looked at him with disdain. "I never want to see you again, Gavin Parringer. Am I clear?"

Her words, coupled with the visual daggers she hurled his way, sliced his heart cleanly in two. She had made her point, and made it with painful clarity. Before he could respond, she whirled around and stormed off toward the house, and presumably, back to her cad of a fiancé. The thought of following her passed through his mind, but he ignored it as his own fury built inside. He had only wanted to help her, to save her from making the biggest mistake of her life, and all he got for his trouble was insults and more rejection.

Well, he'd had enough. He had told her sister, Emily, that he was leaving for a trip abroad, and he would go through with it. If Diana had given him even an inkling that she might have taken his warning to heart he would have cancelled his plans without hesitation. But she'd made her choice and now she had to live with it. He didn't care what she did.

But as he walked back to his townhouse, he knew he would never stop caring, or loving Diana. She was his cross to bear, and always would be. Melancholy strangled him, threatening to squeeze the air from his throat. Perhaps some time in India would help dull the agonizing pain in his heart. Or perhaps not. He had no idea.

What he did know is that he couldn't bear to watch her marry a man who would only hurt her in the end. That right there was enough of a reason to leave England.

Chapter One

May 1820

A chilly London wind cut straight through Gavin Parringer. Shivering, he tugged his overcoat closer to his body. True, the air wasn't all that cold, but the overcast sky, coupled with the fact that he had spent the past eight years in the hot climate of India, made the chill even more acute.

He climbed inside the elegant black carriage assigned to take him to Tamesly House. *His* own personal carriage. He could barely wrap the idea around his head that he owned such a luxurious vehicle. Not when he couldn't remember ever riding in one.

Sinking back in the plush velvet seat, he looked at Dr. Seamus Burns sitting across from him. The only person—the only *thing*—familiar to him since his return to England. The older man pulled his gilded watch out of his pocket, adjusted his spectacles before checking the time, then snapped the watch shut with a click.

The carriage lurched forward. Gavin pulled back the curtain enough so he could look out the window. He drank in every detail of the passing landscape, hoping something would click in his mind. The surrounding buildings ranged from magnificent to needing repair. People were everywhere: walking, riding horses, traveling in carriages and hacks. But nothing looked familiar. Nothing triggered the memories he was so desperate to retrieve. As the carriage passed over a bridge, he stared down into the murky water below.

"The Thames." Seamus leaned forward and pulled open the curtain on his side of the window. "Haven't seen it in years. Hasn't changed a bit, I must say. Still dirty, smelly, and toxic to anyone foolish enough to try to swim in it."

Gavin couldn't imagine why anyone would want to take a dip in the obviously polluted waters. "I should recognize this river, shouldn't I?"

"Aye, lad. You should."

Although at thirty-two Gavin could hardly be called a lad, the good doctor had been addressing him that way for years. Gavin frowned as they left the bridge. He should recognize the Thames. The buildings. The people. Everything.

But he didn't.

He clenched his fists. Frustration he hadn't experienced in more than six years returned full force. "Why can't I remember?" he asked through gritted teeth.

"You know the answer to that, lad."

Gavin shut the curtain tight. "I know the reason, but I thought . . . I had hoped . . ."

Seamus's compassionate expression could easily be seen through the dimness of the coach's interior. He patted Gavin's knee. "You had hoped returning home would trigger your memory. 'Tis a strange thing, amnesia. Some patients fully recover—"

"And some don't." Running his fingers through his hair, Gavin leaned forward. "How long before we arrive?"

"Shouldn't be too long."

"This entire journey has been too long."

"Aye. That I agree with."

Gavin set his elbows on his knees and hung his head. His body swayed with the movement of the carriage. He resisted the urge to pull out the letter he had received a month ago and re-read it, but that wasn't necessary. He knew the contents by heart. The missive had been the impetus for his return to London.

Dear Lord Tamesly,

I hope this letter finds you healthy and well. Allow me to introduce myself. I am Cecil Buttons, the solicitor for your estate. I cannot tell you how happy and relieved I am to discover that you are alive in India. We had feared you dead, for we hadn't heard a word from you since your departure from England eight years ago. I must assure you that I never gave up hope. I spent a considerable amount of personal time and resources to track you down.

Now I must get to the point. Your estate is, unfortunately, in a shambles. I have done the best I can in your absence to take care of your holdings in Lancashire and the family estate in Aberdeen. However, I have faced considerable opposition from your cousin, who has been petitioning the court to declare you deceased, thus acquiring your title and what is left of your estate. Through some intricate legal maneuvering, and with the help of your friend Lord Chesreton, I have been able to keep your cousin from reaching his goal. But I'm afraid that the stalling has come to an end. If you do not return to London posthaste, you will lose everything.

I do not know what has kept you in India, and why you have chosen not to contact me during the last eight years, but I implore you to respond to this letter and let me know what you intend to do.

I remain in your service,
Cecil Buttons, Esq.

Gavin had been shocked to receive the letter, and even more shocked at its contents. For years he had wondered about his past, about the fleeting memories of the life he'd had before the accident. He knew he was from England, since the contrast between him and the people of Calcutta had been glaring. But how he'd gotten to India was a mystery, one even Seamus couldn't help him solve.

Now he at least knew he was a lord of some sort, and owned an estate of unknown value. An estate in trouble, if the letter could be believed. Which Gavin wasn't sure he did. Yet the missive provided more information than he'd ever had before, and it was definitely worth investigating. Fortunately Seamus had offered to accompany him, eager to visit England after a twenty-year absence.

The coach came to a stop and Gavin sat up. The moment of truth had arrived. He would either discover his past or be a victim of a ruse. Either way, his life would never be the same.

"Ready, lad?" Seamus brushed the palm of his hand over the few strands of hair that stretched over his bald pate.

Gavin could tell his friend was forcing himself to remain nonchalant. Seamus was just as curious as he was, perhaps even more so. The man had invested the last eight years of his life, first treating Gavin, then training him to be his assistant. Gavin thought of him as more of a father than a physician. As far as he was concerned, Seamus Burns was the only father he'd ever had.

Nodding, Gavin adjusted the white cravat at his neck. The blasted thing was bloody uncomfortable, but supposedly necessary for a man of his position. He would rather dispense with it altogether, along with the stiff shirt, decorative waistcoat, and form-fitting trousers. Instead he longed for the loose linen pants and long tunic he had in his suitcase. But he felt enough like an outsider. He didn't need to look like one too.

The door opened and he stepped out of the carriage, Seamus not far behind him. The house standing before him was in obvious need of repair. Several of the cobblestones of the drive were loose, rust coated the wrought iron around the small porch, and the window panes were dingy. He could only imagine the condition of the inside.

Suddenly the front door flew open and a tall, blond-haired man with a slender build came bounding toward him.

"Gavin, old chap! You are a sight for sore eyes!" A grin broke out on his face as he gave Gavin a hearty hug.

Out of courtesy Gavin returned the embrace, but with little enthusiasm. He had no idea who this man was—perhaps his cousin? But if that was the case, he wouldn't be all too happy to see him, at least according to what Buttons had said in his letter.

The gent stepped back, his joy tempered by Gavin's lack of response. The man cocked his head to the side and examined his face. "What is it, mate? You look like you've seen a ghost, instead of your best friend."

Ah. So this was Lord Chesreton, the man Cecil spoke of in the letter. Awkward silence filled the moment as Gavin tried to think of what to say. How does one tell his best friend he has no idea who he is?

He was saved from answering when a short, portly man exited the house and made his way toward Gavin, Seamus, and Lord Chesreton. "Lord Tamesly," he said when he reached them. He extended his hand. "Welcome home, my lord. So good to see you after all this time."

Gavin looked at the gentleman. He didn't recognize him either, but he shook his hand. "Thank you," was all he could think of to say.

"And this must be Dr. Burns." The man turned and shook Seamus's hand. "Cecil Buttons, Esquire."

"Pleasure to meet you," Seamus said.

The four men stood on the drive in front of the house, growing more ill at ease. Except for Seamus. Gavin knew he was quietly observing the situation, as was his way.

Cecil and Colin seemed to be waiting for Gavin to take the lead, so he said, "Shall we go inside?"

They expelled a collective sigh of relief, releasing the tension that had built among them all. Colin let out a nervous chuckle. "I took the liberty of pouring us some port from your private stock, Gav. I didn't think you would mind. After all, we have much to celebrate."

"No . . . not at all." Gavin wracked his brain to figure out what port was. A drink, presumably. Seamus's tastes ran between tea and scotch, and when he was particularly stressed he mixed them both. Gavin had refrained from alcohol altogether, preferring to keep his senses as clear as possible. Things were muddy enough as it is.

As they entered the house, his assumption about the disarray of the house had been accurate. He glanced at Cecil, who looked at him sheepishly.

"You have been gone a long time, my lord. I had to dismiss all the servants but one. She has done her best to keep up with everything . . . but it is a large house, as you can see."

Guilt stabbed at him, although he didn't know why. He hadn't neglected his home on purpose. But the thought of people losing their jobs on his account caused a knot to form in his stomach. "It's all right, Mr. Buttons. I know you did what you deemed best."

Cecil's thin lips twitched in a smile. "Thank you, my lord. Shall we adjoin in the study? I hate to plunge right into business matters, but time is of the utmost importance."

Gavin nodded and started to follow Cecil, but Seamus spoke up.

"Gavin, may I have a word?"

Turning around, Gavin looked at his friend, noting his serious expression. He nodded, then turned to Cecil and Lord Chesreton. "Please, go ahead. We will join you shortly." He watched them depart, paying careful attention to the direction they went in. When they both entered a room close by, Gavin let out a breath of relief. The entire situation had been most uncomfortable. He was already starting to regret his decision to return.

"So when are you going to tell them, lad?"

"I don't know!" He rubbed the back of his neck, trying to ease the muscles that had suddenly grown stiff. "Sorry, Seamus, I don't mean to lose my temper with you."

" 'Tis all right. Totally understandable. I am sure I would feel the same way were I in your position." He moved to stand closer to Gavin and lowered his voice. "But you can't hide your condition from them. They already suspect something is wrong. Perhaps you should have prepared them when you replied to Mr. Buttons's letter."

"Perhaps. But I had hoped that once I landed on English soil, everything would have come back to me." He shook his head at his folly. He should have known better. "What should I do now? I can't just walk in that room and tell them I have amnesia."

"Amnesia?"

Both men turned at the sound of Lord Chesreton's voice. The man's mouth had dropped open in shock. "You have no idea who I am?"

Slowly, Gavin shook his head.

Lord Chesreton's brought his hand to his forehead. "Blimey, that explains a lot then, doesn't it? Truth be told I imagined all kinds of scenarios you were involved with while you were gone, but losing your memory wasn't one of them. How long have you had this?"

"Eight years."

"*Eight* years? Since you left London?"

"Yes. At least, I suppose so."

"So you don't even know my name?"

"Other than your title, no. Mr. Buttons did say you were my closest friend." Gavin paused. "Is that true?"

Lord Chesreton strode toward Gavin, then clasped his arm around Gavin's shoulders. "Absolutely. We have known each other since we were tots." The strained look that had been on his face since Gavin's arrival disappeared as he grinned.

For the first time since he'd received the letter, Gavin smiled. He might not remember this man, but he knew he could trust him. If anyone would help him learn about his past, it would be him.

The man led Gavin toward the study. "First off, call me Colin," he said. "Secondly, let's have that port straight away. Seems we're both going to need it."

"Port?" Gavin asked, willing to admit his ignorance now without fear of looking foolish.

Colin threw back his head and laughed. "We have a *lot* of catching up to do!"

Chapter Two

"Diana? Diana! Bother, have you even heard a word I've said?"

Diana turned toward Emily, immediately seeing the frown on her sister's face. They were sitting in Diana's drawing room, taking in the afternoon together. Emily had dropped by for a visit, and she was busily knitting a tiny yellow cap for her new baby as they conversed. But in typical Emily fashion, the stitches were more than a little uneven. Diana didn't dare correct her, however. Emily had been more than a bit touchy in the final months of her pregnancy with her second child.

"I am sorry, Emily. I am afraid my mind wandered a bit. What were you saying?"

Emily sighed. "Honestly, Diana. You have been so

preoccupied lately. Are you sure you are feeling all right?"

"Yes," she responded, facing Emily completely. "I am fine. Please, tell me what you were talking about. I promise I will pay perfect attention this time."

"I hope so," she said with all seriousness. "This does concern your future, you know."

Diana regarded her sister for a moment. She had missed her terribly since Emily and Michael had moved to America six years ago, and had been thrilled when they decided to move back and live in London once again. At the moment they were residing with Colin and Lily, while Michael continued to look for the perfect house for them to live in. Glowing from her pregnancy, blissfully happy with her husband, Michael, and their son, Emily couldn't fathom anyone not being as content as she was. Unfortunately, since Emily's return from America seven months ago, that translated into a couple of matchmaking attempts for Diana that had turned out quite badly.

Immediately sensing that Emily was broaching that sore subject again, she said, "My future is just fine, dear sister."

"I would not call sitting at home on your hands having a future," Emily announced in an all-knowing tone. She set down her knitting and eyed Diana squarely.

"I have been helping Lily with her charity work. I think that should count for something."

"Of course it does," Emily said quickly. "You know I admire all the volunteering you're involved in. Hopefully I can help in some capacity after the baby is born."

Diana smiled. "What a wonderful idea! Lily and I would love to have you."

"Thank you. I shall seriously consider it. But darling, I am not talking about your philanthropy, as fantastic as that is." She took a deep breath, as if measuring her next words. "I know you still miss William, but do you not think it is high time for you to, well, get back into the game, so to speak?"

A knot formed in Diana's stomach. "Into the game?"

"The matrimony game, of course."

Diana couldn't believe what she was hearing. True, she had been widowed for over four years, but that didn't mean she was ready to get married again. And after her disastrous marriage to William, she didn't want to. However, no one knew what the true state of her union with William had been. She kept the pain her late husband had caused a secret from everyone, including her family. Keeping up the ruse, she said, "Even though I miss William—"

Her sister's face split into a satisfied smile.

"—that does not mean I am not perfectly fine with the way things are. Because I am."

"Balderdash!" Emily replied. "If you are so happy,

then why do you look tired all the time? I can see the shadows under your eyes right now."

Diana touched the tender skin beneath her lower eyelid. She had been tired as of late and hadn't been sleeping well. But she was entitled to a bit of insomnia every once in a while, wasn't she?

"Dear sister, I know you. I know you must be lonely, especially for someone as social as you are. To be spending so much time by yourself, alone . . . it must be so sad. I know I would feel the same way if I did not have my Michael."

With a sigh, Diana looked away. "You are very lucky to have him," she said softly.

"Oh, Diana, I'm so sorry. I surely did not mean to make you upset. That was completely insensitive of me."

"Do not worry about it, Emily." Diana smiled to show she knew Emily's words had been said only out of concern and not spitefulness.

Emily glanced at her crooked knitting and wrung her hands together. "Oh, bother, Michael is right. I do seem to run at the mouth more than I should. Especially with this pregnancy." Her head shot up, a stricken expression on her face. "Blast, I did it again."

Throughout the afternoon Diana had tried to stem the pang of jealousy over her sister's impending motherhood, but she had failed, and Emily must have picked up on it. Absently she touched her flat stomach. Would she ever experience the joy of motherhood? She doubted it.

"Diana? Oh, dear, I have really done it this time, haven't I?"

While she might feel jealous over not having a child of her own, Diana could never hold it against Emily. In fact, she was thrilled her sister was having another baby. She adored her brother Colin's daughter, Clarissa, and Emily's son, Michael, and she couldn't wait to shower affection over the new addition to Emily and Michael's family. She gave her sister a reassuring smile. "Emily, please, do not worry about it. I am not offended in the least."

Her sister sighed with relief. "You are most understanding, dear heart. Perhaps one day I will learn to measure my words before I speak them aloud."

"And deprive us of your straightforwardness? I won't hear of it."

Giggling, Emily relaxed. "Oh, all right then. I do hate to disappoint."

"Good." Diana then sobered, her thoughts suddenly taking a serious tack. "Emily, I will grant you that I have been having trouble sleeping as of late."

"Then we should do something about it!"

"We?"

Emily leaned forward, shifting her pregnant frame in the chair until she found a comfortable position. "Ruby is having a party this Friday eve. You should come."

Diana shook her head. Perhaps she had been too agreeable with her sister. She had avoided most parties in the past four years since her husband's death, although she had attended a musicale two weeks ago. But she didn't want to make it a regular habit. At least not anymore. "Really, Emily, I am not interested—"

"A *small* party, just close family and friends. I know my mother-in-law would love it if you would come, as would Michael and I. And Colin and Lily, not to mention our mother—"

"I get the point." Diana straightened the folds of her light blue dress. She'd been told this color brought out the blue in her eyes, and she had worn it to many a party when she was younger. Now she wore the color because of the serviceability of the dress, not because it accentuated her looks.

Emily frowned and moved around in the chair again. "Bugger, I can never get comfortable enough." She made one more change in position, then gave up. "I just do not understand you, Diana. You used to love to go to parties. Remember when you were the belle of the ball? All the men could not wait to dance with you, to court you . . ." Her voice trailed off wistfully.

She remembered it keenly, and her cheeks always heated at the memories. Years ago she'd never miss an opportunity to socialize, especially with members of the opposite sex. She had been aware of her popularity, and found particular pleasure in cultivating it. In fact, she and her friend Henrietta had often held contests between them to see who could collect the most gentlemen callers. Diana usually won. When she thought about how many men she'd strung along, with little regard of their feelings—suffice it to say she was more than happy that behavior was a part of her past. "Fortunately for all concerned, I have outgrown that time of my life, Emily."

"One can never outgrow having fun, Diana."

"Depends on what one considers fun."

Emily huffed. "You are determined to vex me, are you not?"

Diana let out a light chuckle. "Yes, dear sister. Vexing you is at the top of my list. I have so missed it while you and Michael were gone."

"Fine. You can be as stubborn as you want, *after* the party."

"You are not going to let this go, are you?"

"No. And if you want to know how stubborn *I* can be, just ask Michael. I am sure he will have more than a few tales to tell you."

"Tales of woe, no doubt." Diana's mouth crooked into a half-smile. "All right. I acquiesce. I will go to the party."

"Fantastic! Michael and I will pick you up thirty minutes beforehand. Now, I am afraid I must be getting home. Michael will be wondering where I am. He can be too overprotective at times." With effort, Emily stood from her chair. She waddled over to Diana, bent over, and kissed her sister's cheek. "You will have a good time, I promise you that."

Diana looked up at her. "I only want one promise from you, Emily. I do not want you to play match-maker for me anymore. That includes at this party. I do not mind spending time with my family, but I have no desire to have a suitor, no matter how *suitable* you think he is."

Pushing back a wayward lock of blond hair, Emily sniffed. "You just insulted me . . . I think. Oh, all right. Have it your way. I doubt there will be any prospects at the party anyway, considering it is just a small gath-ering. But at least you will be around other people, in-stead of walled up in this empty house of yours."

"Thank you for being concerned." Diana ignored Emily's latest lack of tact and stood and hugged her sister, not an easy feat with Emily's swelling belly between them. "I appreciate your worrying about me. And I promise I will go right to bed after you leave and catch up on my sleep."

"You had better."

Emily left shortly thereafter, but not before re-minding Diana what time she and Michael would be by on Friday, which was only two days away. "You had better start figuring out which one of your gor-

geous gowns you plan to wear," she added before
walking out the door.

After her sister left, Diana sat in the high-backed
chair in the sitting room and stared at the embers dying in the fireplace, her ball gowns the furthest from
her mind. Her mother had tried to convince her to
move back home after William died, but Diana hadn't
wanted to. She and William had lived separate lives for
the last two years of their marriage, and she had forged
a life of her own. She liked her independence, and it
served her well. However, there were moments like
this, when she faced the rest of the evening alone, that
she had to admit Emily was correct. She was lonely.
She had been lonely for such a long time, even when
William was alive.

But being matched with some random man—no
matter his pedigree or coffers—wasn't the answer to
her loneliness, despite Emily's vocal opinion on the
matter. She was finished with marriage and men. Living alone was preferable to a match of convenience,
which would be the only type of marriage she would
have. She would not allow herself to fall in love
again, only to be betrayed. Men only valued her for
her looks, they always had. She had thought William
would be different, but he had considered her more of
a trophy than a wife. And when he had no use for her
anymore . . .

She shivered, physically shaking off the memories

of his betrayal. No, despite bouts of loneliness and envy over the perfect marriages her siblings have, she preferred living alone over a broken heart.

Of that she was sure.

Chapter Three

Two days after his arrival in London, Gavin studied the row of austere paintings lining the wall of the drawing room in his unfamiliar house. They were a family tree of sorts, starting with the original Lord Tamesly in 1727. Gavin focused on each portrait, trying to reach deep in the recesses of his mind for any shred of memory of his ancestors. By the time he got to his father, he had given up.

Still, he felt drawn to the man's portrait, which had to mean something. He could see parts of himself in the painting—he had his father's green eyes and dark hair. But Gavin couldn't relate to the man's severe expression. Had his father always been so intimidating? Or had the painter taken artistic liberties? Blast, he wished he could remember.

His father's portrait was the last one in the row. At least that was what Gavin had thought, and he had even started to move away from the gallery until something interesting caught his eye. He moved closer to examine the empty space next to his father. There it was, a slight, but detectable difference in the shading of the wallpaper.

There had been a portrait there before.

Most puzzling. Gavin assumed the picture was of him, but he couldn't be quite sure, since of course he didn't recall ever having his portrait painted. There was only one way to find out. He rang for Jocelyn Bloomfield, the housemaid, and the last servant who had remained in his employ during his absence.

"Yes, m'lord?" The gray-haired woman gave him a short curtsy. She looked to be in her sixties, and from the stiffness of her movements, he suspected she was in some sort of pain.

"It must have been very hard to fulfill your duties by yourself," he said, a pang of guilt stabbing at him.

"I have managed, my lord." She lifted her chin, her expression filled with pride. "Have I failed you in some way? If I have, I promise to do better."

Gavin shook his head. "No, no, not at all. You have done splendid work here, Mrs. Bloomfield. I could not be more satisfied with how well you have managed, especially with so little assistance. I am sorry you have had to carry such a burden for so long." Even though the house was in desperate need of a do-over, she had done a magnificent job of keeping the place clean and tidy. Yet he couldn't expect one servant, a woman well into her dotage at that, to do any more than she'd already done.

Her defensive expression faded slightly. "Thank you, my lord. I am happy you are pleased with my work." She gave him a small smile. "Was there something you wanted?"

"Yes." He moved back to the reason he summoned her. "Over here, on the wall next to my father's portrait. Was there another painting here?"

Mrs. Bloomfield nodded, pushing her wire-rimmed glasses further up her nose. "Your cousin Percival requested it be removed."

"And who was the painting of?"

"Why, you, my lord, of course. I pleaded with him not to take it down, even though he insisted that you were . . . dead." She glanced away for a moment, then looked at him again. "But he wouldn't hear of it, even when I pointed out that at the very least out of respect your portrait should remain."

Rubbing his chin, Gavin asked, "How long ago did this occur?"

"A few months ago."

"Do you know what happened to the painting?"

"No, my lord. He took it down himself, then left the house. I do not know what he did with it." Moving toward him, she lowered her voice. "Pardon me for saying this, but I do not trust the man. He is shifty, if you know what I mean."

Gavin nodded, but he had to take her at her word, considering he didn't remember Percival at all. But he did think it was strange that his cousin would go to the trouble to remove his portrait. There seemed no point in doing so.

"Is there anything else, my lord?"

"No, Mrs. Bloomfield, you have been a great help."

"Thank you, my lord."

She curtsied again, then turned to leave, only to stop when Gavin called her name.

"I think it high time I hire some more staff to take the burden off of you. As soon as I can sort through my business affairs, I will start the hiring process."

She smiled freely, tears shining in her eyes. "Your doctor friend told me what happened to you in India. About you losing your memory." She walked closer to him. "You may not have your memories, my lord, but you have not lost your fine character, or your kind nature, thank the good Lord." Turning quickly, she rushed out of the room.

Gavin pressed his lips together in a half-grin at the unexpected compliment. Perhaps things here wouldn't be so difficult after all.

"I suppose you are wondering why I have asked you all here today."

Diana watched as her brother, Colin, paced the width of his study in front of his large mahogany desk. He seemed uncharacteristically discomfited, possibly because he rarely ever called a family meeting. Dread formed inside her. Something must be terribly wrong.

The entire family filled the study, with the exception of seven-year-old Clarissa and little Michael, who were with Clarissa's governess. Lily, Colin's wife and Clarissa's mother, sat on the settee in the middle of the room, her slim face appearing equally disconcerted. Elizabeth, Diana's mother, perched beside her. Emily and Michael sat in the loveseat, his arm resting lightly over her shoulders. He rubbed the top of his wife's shoulder with his fingers in a small, but tender, gesture. Despite the casualness of his appearance, everyone seemed to be on edge.

Colin stopped pacing and looked at all of them. Sensing their apprehension, he relaxed his stance. "The world has not come to an end, if that is what you are all worried about."

"Of course it has not, Colin. Do not be ridiculous." Elizabeth removed her spectacles and wiped the lenses with a linen monogrammed handkerchief. "But I must say your behavior has us a bit concerned. Especially since you are acting quite secretive all of the sudden."

A few concurring murmurs resounded in the room.

Colin held up his hands, palms facing outward. "There is nothing wrong, I assure you. In fact, I have good news. I simply wanted to tell everyone at once, to make things easier. This way I do not have to repeat the information a dozen times or so."

Elizabeth clapped her hands together. "Oh, darling, I just knew it! You are expecting!" She reached over and grabbed Lily in a huge hug, causing Lily to nearly jump out of her seat in surprise.

Diana watched Lily flick a confused look at her husband.

Colin's face turned a light crimson shade. "Er, no, mother. Lily is not expecting."

"Most *definitely* not," Lily added, giving her mother-in-law a consoling pat on the arm.

"Oh." Elizabeth slowly retreated back to her seat, her tone and facial expression betraying her awkwardness. "Pardon my mistake."

Diana felt a bit embarrassed for her mother, yet she wasn't surprised that she had jumped to that conclusion. Elizabeth Dymoke was perhaps the most doting grandmother in London, and had made it quite clear she would adore a few more grandchildren, because three was hardly enough.

Casting a quick glance at Emily, she saw her sister pretending to smooth invisible wrinkles in her skirt. She then observed Michael, who by the spark in his eyes, obviously found the scene quite amusing. Emily elbowed him lightly in the ribs.

"But know this, Mother," Colin said quickly, trying to diffuse the increasingly tense situation. "If we are expecting, you will be the first person we inform."

"Well, I should hope so," Elizabeth said, looking a bit mollified at the smallest hint that she might have another grandchild someday.

"Absolutely. Now that we've cleared that up, we should get to the business at hand." Colin leaned against his desk, slipping his hands into his trouser pockets. "Gavin Parringer is back in London."

Diana mouth dropped open. She had never thought to hear his name again. Painful memories instantly flooded through her.

"Considering that Gavin's relationship with our family is a bit . . . complicated," Colin looked at Emily first, then Diana, "I wanted to tell you the news myself, before you heard it through London's gossip vine."

Diana couldn't help but look at Emily, who seemed as shocked as she was. But Michael's response was quite different. He immediately tensed, his expression turning to granite, his body appearing ready to spring from the loveseat at any moment. His response wasn't surprising, considering his wife had been in love with Gavin at one time, albeit before Emily and Michael were romantically involved.

But Gavin's affections hadn't resided with Emily. He had been in love with someone else.

With me.

A huge stab of guilt went through her. Gavin had been one of many men who had pledged his love to her in the past, and who she had treated with very little regard. She wasn't clueless about her beauty, and in her youth she had done everything she could to not only enhance it, but to use it to her advantage. Gavin's declarations of love, while she thought sweet at the time, were only part of many such announcements she'd heard from single gentlemen of the *ton.*

Then she met William, and everything changed. She became engaged, and Gavin had tried to warn her about him. She had dismissed him outright, and he had disappeared. She'd heard he'd left for India, but she hadn't heard from him since. She vaguely remembered there being some gossip about him being missing, but truthfully she hadn't thought about him much at all, especially after marrying William. She hadn't wanted to think about him, to think how different her life would have been if she had only heeded his warnings. Instead she had, in her characteristically vain and unfeeling way, cast him aside and told him she never wanted to see him again. That decision had changed her life forever. If only she had listened to him . . .

"So he has decided to come back to England," Michael said, still looking tense. "Things not going well for him in India, I presume."

"Actually, that is not the case at all," Colin responded. "For the past few years, I was not even sure he was in India. No one had heard a word from him after he left England."

"Really?" Emily leaned forward and out from under Michael's arm. "Not a single word?"

"It was as if he had disappeared completely."

"Then what happened to him while he was gone?"

Colin frowned. "Well, we are not completely sure."

"We?" Michael asked.

"Cecil Buttons, Gavin's solicitor, and myself. Gavin's cousin has been trying to have him declared dead for nearly eight years, but Buttons and I refused to give up. Somehow we both knew Gavin was still alive. Call it a gut feeling, if you will. Finally, nearly three months ago, Buttons' investigative man found him in Calcutta. Buttons then contacted him. But when he came back . . ." Colin shook his head. "Let us just say he is not the same bloke who left London eight years ago."

"What do you mean?" Emily queried, ignoring her husband's growing annoyance with her obvious interest in Gavin. "How is he not the same?"

"He has lost his memory. Amnesia, his doctor-friend called it. He remembers nothing about his past. He had no idea who I was when I met up with him a couple days ago. Did not even recognize his own flat. It was the strangest thing to witness."

"Poor man," Lily said, shaking her head. "Is there anything we can do to help?"

"That is another reason why I wanted to talk to all of you. I thought maybe if he were around close friends, that might trigger some of his memories. His doctor is not quite convinced that it will work, but he was not against the idea either. Reuniting Gavin with those he knew best would not be a bad thing at all."

"I am not so sure about that," Michael mumbled.

Emily looked at him. "What do you mean by that? Of course we can help him. He has no one else, except for that dreadful cousin of his—what is the man's name?"

"Percival Parringer," Colin supplied.

Diana shuddered at the mention of Gavin's cousin. She had reluctantly attended few parties since her husband's death, but the last party she went to Percival was there. He asked her to dance numerous times, and when she finally agreed, he made no mystery of his interest in pursuing her further. He was an oily, unattractive man who perspired entirely too much and had the manners of a lout. That he and Gavin were related was hard to fathom.

"He is next in line for the title, thus his eagerness to have Gavin declared dead. And you are right, Emily, he is a poor excuse for a man. Gav certainly does not need that kind of chap in his life, especially right now."

"Agreed." Emily nodded with satisfaction. "We should invite him for supper posthaste."

"Wait just a minute." Michael sprang up from his chair. "Am I the only person who remembers how much trouble this bloke caused?" He looked from Emily to Diana, then back to his wife again.

"You are overreacting, dear," Emily said, looking up at her husband.

"Overreacting? I hardly think being concerned that the man my wife used to be in love with—who used to be in love with her sister, I should add—might cause a bit of a problem or two for all of us."

"Michael . . . ooof . . . ," Emily said as she struggled to get to her feet. "Bother, will you help me get up off this settee?"

He leaned over and helped Emily stand. She smoothed back a couple strands of blond hair in an effort to reclaim her dignity. Stepping toward her husband, she said in hushed tones, "Darling, so much has changed since Gavin was last here. Trust me, my love, you have nothing to worry about."

"I am sorry, sweetheart, but I cannot help but be protective, especially when it comes to him. I remember what he did to you."

"Michael, that was in the past. You are my present, my future." She took his hand and kissed his fingers. "I will say it again, you have nothing to worry about. Whatever I felt for Gavin was nothing compared to what I feel for you."

Diana felt like an intruder as she watched her sister reassure Michael that whatever feelings she had for Gavin were completely gone. After a few more whispered words, they both sat down, Michael's confident expression returning. He leaned over and kissed her on the cheek.

Colin cleared his throat, signaling that Diana wasn't the only one who felt like a voyeur. Yet the tender scene had a calming effect on everyone, and they all visibly relaxed.

"I think your idea of inviting Gavin for dinner is a smashing one, Emily." Lily said, smiling. "I shall send the invitation to him this afternoon."

"He should come to your mother's party as well," Emily interjected, looking at Michael.

He hesitated for a moment, then finally nodded in agreement. "I will mention it to her tonight when we go visit."

Emily beamed at Michael, which caused him to grin in return. Clearly he would do anything in his power to make his wife happy.

"Then that settles it," Colin said, a smile of satisfaction crossing his face. "I really think once Gavin is among friends he will start regaining the memories he has lost. I can't imagine what the poor chap has gone through, not knowing who he was or where he came from, living in a foreign country for all those years." He shook his head. "It is truly hard to fathom. I just hope we can help him."

A few moments later, after the details of the supper were ironed out, everyone left the study, Diana exiting last. She turned at the sound of Colin calling her name.

"Did you need something else, Colin?" she asked.

He strode toward her and stopped when they were face to face. "I just wanted to make sure you were all right with all this." He put his hands on her shoulders. "I do not want to make things awkward for you. If you would like, you can choose not to be here when we have Gavin over for supper. No one would blame you in the least. But I really think your presence would be of great help to him."

Eyeing him warily, she asked, "Why?"

"Because he was in love with you, Diana." Colin dropped his hands and leaned back against his desk again. "I remember when he told me about it. He was completely besotted. He had an emotional connection to you."

Diana averted her eyes. Colin knew so little about what had really happened between them, and she had to keep it that way. "Unfortunately, it was one-sided. I feel horrible about that."

"You should not. He knew he could not force you to love him. Knowing Gavin, he never would have wanted to coerce you into anything."

She nodded. "I know he would not. He was a fine man."

"He still is."

Turning away, she thought for a moment. Then she asked, "Do you really think I can help him?"

"Yes, I do."

Uncertainty filled her. She knew it would be unwise

to get involved with Gavin again, despite her sympathy for his plight. Not to mention the terrible way she had treated him the last time they were together. Yet she couldn't help but feel that this was a second chance of sorts, an opportunity for her to make amends, something she desperately needed and wanted to do. She hesitated for a long moment, then made her decision. "I shall be here. I want him to regain his memory as much as you do. And I also do not want any unpleasantness between us. I am sure whatever feelings Gavin had for me in the past are long gone, and would be even if his memories were still intact."

"I am not so sure about that. He cared for you probably more than you realize."

"That was a long time ago, Colin. As Emily has said, things have changed. I think we should focus on helping Gavin, not on worrying about what happened in the past."

Colin grinned, then leaned over and kissed Diana's cheek. "You are a prime woman, sister of mine. Thank you for your selflessness."

Diana didn't consider herself very selfless, and if her brother had been privy to the last conversation she'd had with Gavin, she knew he wouldn't think she was either. But she appreciated that her brother thought she was. Despite what had happened between her and Gavin, she needed to help him.

Even if in the course of prompting him to remember his life he remembered how she treated him.

She put the worry out of her mind. Now was the time to focus on helping Gavin, not think about her own personal welfare. She would deal with the fallout when it happened.

Which it would. She had no doubt about that.

Chapter Four

Gavin arrived at Colin's home a few minutes earlier than specified in the invitation Colin's wife, Lady Dymoke, had sent. He had asked Seamus to accompany him, but the doctor had declined, saying he thought it better if Gavin were immersed with his friends rather than using him as an emotional crutch. The older man planned a quiet dinner inside Gavin's flat, catching up on his reading. But Gavin sorely missed his reassuring presence. Here, sitting in the carriage and looking at the stately manor before him, he felt more than a little apprehensive.

Finally, he could stall no longer. He stepped out of his vehicle and waved his driver off. The man would return for him at a later time.

Gavin took in the splendid scene before him—the

perfectly manicured lawn, the colorful English roses climbing up the trellis, and the polished stone steps leading up the house. With more than a little trepidation, he rang the doorbell.

In short order a tall, wiry man with a pointy nose opened the door. "Yes?" he inquired in a stuffy, long drawl.

"I am here to see Colin," Gavin said, trying not to be intimidated by the butler's unyielding presence. "Pardon me, I mean Lord Dymoke."

"You are Lord Tamesly, I presume?"

"Yes," he said, relieved the man knew he was an expected guest.

The butler opened the door wider. "Please come in. I will inform Lord and Lady Dymoke of your arrival."

"Thank you," Gavin said as he stepped into the house. He walked through the doorway and stood in the foyer as the butler left to seek out Colin. Looking at the splendor around him—marble floors, gilded finials, and a glittering gigantic chandelier suspended from the ceiling—he nodded his approval. Impressive, indeed, and far removed from the wreck that was his own abode. Just today he had started tabulating how much the repairs and updates would cost him.

During their last visit together, Colin had told him about his wife, Lily, along with the rest of his family. He had two sisters—Diana, a widow, and Emily, who was married to a bloke named Michael. They had sounded like a delightful bunch, and he wished his memory banks held even a snippet of any of them. But he had no idea about his friend's family. In fact, if one of them ran right into him, he wouldn't know who they were.

"Michael! Michael, where are you?"

A young, female child burst into the foyer. Gavin estimated she was no older than seven. She possessed luminous dark-blond curls, and large brown eyes fringed with the longest lashes he'd ever seen on a little girl. The tot was positively adorable.

"Oh," she said, stopping in her tracks. Immediately she clutched her light blue skirt and gave him a small, but perfectly executed, curtsy. "I am sorry, I did not know we had a visitor."

Considering the adult tone of her statement, Gavin thought he'd erred in guessing her age. She spoke and carried herself as if she were a much older child.

"I am Clarissa Dymoke," she said. "I was looking for my cousin, Michael. We are playing hide and seek, and I am afraid he has hidden himself quite well."

Ah, Colin and Lily's daughter. He should have seen the resemblance to her father. Utterly charmed, Gavin bowed slightly at the waist. "Pleasure to make your acquaintance, Miss Dymoke. I am Lord Tamesly, a . . . uh, . . . long time friend of your father's."

"You know my father?" She smiled. "Odd, he has not mentioned you before."

"I have been away for a long time. Overseas, actually."

Her eyes widened. "How exciting! My uncle Michael and aunt Emily used to live overseas as well, but they moved back to London from America a few months ago. Are you from there as well?"

"Wrong sea, I am afraid. I lived in India for a time."

Clarissa's expression reflected her confusion. "I do not know much about India. I imagine I will learn about it from my tutor. Maybe I will even travel there someday."

"Maybe you will." Gavin grinned. Blast if he didn't feel as if he was having a conversation with a twenty-year-old.

"Do you know my aunt and uncle?" she asked.

"I did at one time," he replied. "But it has been a while since we spoke last."

"What about my aunt Diana?"

Gavin frowned and, for the millionth time, inwardly cursed his amnesia. "I am afraid I do not," he said, believing it ridiculous to lie to a child.

"Are you married?"

The forthright question caught him off guard. "No. Why do you ask?"

She fluttered her pale blond eyelashes at him. "My auntie Diana isn't married either. Although she used to be, until her husband died a few years ago. I know my auntie Emily wants her to find someone soon. She thinks she is lonely."

"I am sorry to hear that."

"I think she hides it well." Clarissa twirled one of

her shoulder length curls. "She certainly does not like when my aunt Emily meddles in her affairs."

He struggled to maintain a serious expression. He was learning more from this precocious child than anyone he'd met in London so far. "Is that a fact?"

"Yes, it is." She cocked her head to the side. "Did my aunt Emily invite you for supper? My auntie Diana is here, and she usually does not come for supper."

"No, your father invited me. We are old friends, remember?"

"Oh, yes, that is right. I had just thought for a moment that you were another one of Auntie Emily's matchmaking projects. Oh, there you are, Michael."

Gavin looked to see a chubby little boy toddle into the foyer from the side entry. He stared up at him with mild curiosity, then made his way toward Clarissa.

"Where the devil have you been?" she asked.

"Clarissa!" Colin entered the room and gave his daughter a stern look. "Young ladies do *not* use such language!"

She looked contrite. "Yes, Father."

"I see you have met Lord Tamesly." Colin gave him an apologetic look. "I hope my daughter has not talked your ear off. She rather enjoys conversing."

"She is a delight." Gavin smiled at the little girl. "I have thoroughly enjoyed meeting you, Miss Clarissa."

Clarissa's cheeks reddened. "My goodness, you are a charmer."

"Clarissa!" Colin sounded on the verge of exasperation.

Gavin laughed. "Why, thank you, young lady. I consider that an extreme compliment, coming from such a charming young lady as yourself."

Colin, apparently not finding his daughter quite as delightful as Gavin did, said, "Why don't you and Michael run along. I am sure your mother is looking for you."

"Yes, Father." She executed another perfect curtsy.

"And tell her that Lord Tamesly has arrived."

She nodded, then took Michael's small hand in hers and led him down the hallway.

"Sorry about that," Colin said, looking at Gavin. "I love her to bits, but she can be a bit much."

"I will say I have learned a lot about your sisters."

A strange expression crossed his features. "What did my daughter tell you?"

"Just that Emily—that is her name, correct?"

Colin nodded.

"Emily and her husband just returned from America after an extended stay there. Also that your other sister is a widow." He chuckled.

Frowning, Colin said, "I fail to find how that information is funny, Gavin."

Realizing his faux pas, Gavin quickly corrected himself. "No, of course that's not funny. Pardon my insensitivity. What I did find amusing is that Clarissa thought I was here at Emily's behest. Apparently she has been playing the matchmaker for Diana."

"Oh." Colin looked less troubled now, but Gavin still didn't fully comprehend the strange mood that had suddenly come over his friend. "Did she mention anything else?"

"No. That was pretty much the entire conversation."

Something akin to relief washed over Colin's face. "Well, then, I will apologize once more for Clarissa's penchant to spill the family's business."

"No apologies necessary."

"I shall have to speak to her about discretion. It is high time she learned some. Shall we proceed to the dining room? I am sure Lily and our cook have created a splendid meal."

The scent of roasted lamb wafted into Gavin's nose several feet before he and Colin had reached the dining room. Gavin's stomach growled as they walked into the room and took in the magnificent feast before them. This was more food than he'd seen in many years. His diet had been sparse in Calcutta, mostly out of necessity, and partly because he had never quite developed a taste for Indian cuisine.

Around the long, polished mahogany table sat several people. His gaze landed on an older, regal-looking woman, her upswept dark-blond hair threaded with silver. Colin's mother, he presumed. Next to her sat a thin woman with plain brown hair who appeared to be close to his age. Her appearance was unremarkable, until she smiled at him. The movement made her face glow with radiance, and gave her a soft, sophisticated beauty. As her seat was next to the empty one at the end of the table, he assumed the woman was Colin's wife, Lily.

Across from Lily sat a rather overdressed man who resembled the young toddler Gavin had met moments before. Beside him was a sweet-faced woman clearly in the late stages of pregnancy. Auntie Emily, perhaps?

"Please excuse my tardiness, everyone," a delicate, feminine voice sounded from behind Gavin.

He spun around. When he looked at the woman the voice belonged to, his heart stopped beating.

Never had he seen such a beautiful woman in his life.

He was staring, but at that moment manners and good sense weren't exactly at the forefront of his mind. Her skin was as smooth and refined as priceless porcelain, with the most perfect rosy tint on her cheeks. Her blue eyes were bluer than the Mediterranean Sea, and her slim figure curved in the most perfect places. The word stunning didn't do her justice.

At the sound of Colin clearing his throat, Gavin reluctantly pulled his gaze away from the lovely woman. Colin immediately moved and stood by her. His stance, oddly enough, was protective. Gavin wondered why.

"Hello, Gavin," the woman said, giving him a tentative smile.

Her voice sent soothing waves over his body. She

looked up at him, her eyes endless blue pools. He couldn't help but get lost in them.

"Do you remember me, Gavin?" she asked. "I am Diana, Colin's sister."

No, he didn't remember her. Bother, but he was in a bad way if he could forget this lovely creature standing in front of him. He remembered Clarissa's words about him being a possible matchmaking target for Diana. Now that he had seen her . . . he couldn't help but wish for a brief moment that the child's assumption had been right.

Diana took her time cutting the tender lamb into tiny pieces, trying to ignore Gavin's gaze on her. He had been staring at her for most of the meal, although she could tell by the way he kept averting his gaze he tried to hide his interest. It was all very strange. In one way he was acting much the same as he had when they had first met—keenly interested in her. On the other hand, he clearly had no memory of ever meeting her before. Very odd indeed.

She took a bite of the meat, savoring its rich, spicy taste. The cook in Colin's employ always prepared delicious fare. Poor Isabel, for whom her mother had some sort of inexplicable loyalty to, had yet to conquer even the most basic of culinary arts, despite years of working as the Dymoke's family cook. Diana always enjoyed taking a meal at her sister-in-law's house.

Usually she felt comfortable and quite at ease. Except for now. Everyone around the table was uncharacteristically quiet.

"Delicious supper," Emily piped up, echoing Diana's thoughts about the meal. Having cleared her plate, she reached for another serving of bread. "Just a bit more." A small, guilty smile played on her lips.

"You're eating for two, darling." Elizabeth handed her another slice of bread. "No need to starve yourself—or apologize."

"Yes, but lately it's been as if I've been eating for three."

"Perhaps you are." Elizabeth clasped her hands together, her eyes wide with excitement over the prospect of having two more grandchildren for the price of one. "Twins! Now darling, wouldn't that be fantastic?"

"Yes," Diana and Lily said at once.

"No!" Emily and Michael said at the same time. Michael added, "One baby at a time, if you please. Especially since our son is barely out of his nappies."

Diana couldn't help but glance at Gavin, who had his head down as he maintained his focus on his empty dish. Normally this type of conversation wouldn't have caused her any discomfiture, especially among her family members. They had always been rather open and found great joy in causing each other consternation, especially Colin and Emily. In the past Gavin had even been privy to more than one personal conversation between one set of family members or another. Yet he seemed very uncomfortable at the moment, as if he were an outsider looking in.

But if her mother realized that, she didn't let on. Instead, she continued in the same vein. "Tsk, tsk," she said, looking at Emily over the rim of her teacup before taking a delicate sip. She set the cup down. "If you have twins, you'll have plenty of help. What with me and Lily and Diana at your beck and call—"

"I don't think Lily appreciates you volunteering for her," Colin interjected.

Lily patted her husband's arm. "Nonsense. You know I'm happy to help Emily. She was my best friend before she became my sister-in-law, after all."

Elizabeth gave Colin a satisfied look before turning her attention back to Emily. "See, darling. With our assistance you could even have triplets without any problem."

"Perish the thought," Michael muttered.

Everyone, including Gavin this time, laughed. Diana was glad he had finally become a little more comfortable among them. She decided to draw him further into the conversation, but away from the topic at hand. "Tell us, Gavin, did you have any interesting adventures in India?"

"Well," he said, pausing to put down his fork. "I do believe losing my memory was quite an adventure."

Diana started to blush at asking such an obvious

question, but then saw the glint in his eyes. He was teasing, and she couldn't help but return a smile.

"But to answer your question in a serious manner, once I recovered from my accident—"

"You had an accident?" Emily's eyes shone with interest. "Is that how you lost your memory?"

Gavin nodded. "I believe so. I can only go on what Seamus—Dr. Burns—told me. He did not know what happened to me exactly, just that he found me on the docks with a terrific gash on my head and not knowing who I was or how I had gotten there. He brought me back to his clinic."

"How dreadful," Elizabeth said, patting the corner of her mouth with her linen napkin. She placed the cloth back on her lap and looked at Gavin with interest.

"Yes, it was. I have to admit it is frustrating in the extreme not to remember one's own history." He paused, then glanced around at everyone at the table. "Although I must have very good taste, for I had the good fortune of being friends with all of you."

Normally Diana would have scoffed at this bit of buttering up, but the words were said with such sincerity, they touched her deep inside. He looked at her for a moment and an inexplicably warm shiver ran down her spine as their gazes locked.

Good heavens! Where did that spark come from?

But it didn't make any sense. She knew Gavin, had been courted by him, yet had never reacted to him in such a way before. Why was she having these emotions now, eight years after his return? Perhaps her sister had been correct—she was lonelier than she thought.

"After Seamus nursed me back to health," Gavin continued, "I began helping him in his clinic, and we worked well together. We also developed a friendship. So I do think that losing my memory has been beneficial, in that I made a very good friend."

"My lord?"

All heads turned as the butler, Hughes, entered the room.

"Yes," Colin said.

"Pardon the interruption, but I have a message for Lord Tamesly. It was just delivered a few moments ago."

Gavin rose from the table and met the taller man, who handed him a piece of paper. He scanned it quickly, then folded it and put it in his pocket. "I am gravely sorry, but I must take my leave. It seems my cousin has just returned from abroad, and is requesting he see me. Immediately."

Diana saw a tiny muscle in Gavin's cheek jerk. He didn't seem happy at all with the prospect of seeing his cousin. She could hardly blame him.

"Thank you for your hospitality, Lily." He walked over to her and kissed her cheek. "I do hope we can do this another time."

"Absolutely, Gavin. Thank you for coming. It is so good to have you back."

"Yes, Gavin," Emily said, smiling. "We are all happy you have returned."

His grin might have been for Emily, but when Diana saw it her insides turned to porridge. He had the most marvelously appealing smile. How could she not have noticed it before?

For the first time, she understood why her sister had fallen in love with Gavin Parringer.

Chapter Five

As Gavin retrieved his coat, he fought to tamp down his irritation at his cousin. His note had said it was imperative that they meet, but Gavin thought it poor form that the man couldn't wait until he was at least finished with supper before summoning him. Percival had not only interrupted a delicious meal, he had also put an end to what had turned out to be a delightful evening.

But more importantly, he had taken him away from the enchanting Diana Garland.

Gavin still couldn't believe he didn't remember anything about her. How could one forget such beauty, grace, and refined dignity? Not to mention a good sense of humor. She was as quick-witted as her brother and sister, a trait he appreciated. He seriously doubted he would enjoy his cousin's company one-tenth as much.

He had more than a niggling of discomfiture at the thought of his cousin. The feeling didn't just stem from the fact that Percival had taken his portrait down from the wall. Truly, he didn't really care if his picture was in the gallery or not, although he did get a sense that it should be there in respect to tradition. No, the niggle was deeper, just out of reach, as if his subconscious were trying to tell him something about Percival.

Or trying to warn him.

"Your coat, my lord." Hughes handed him the light-weight jacket.

Gavin slipped it on. "Thank you," he said.

The butler nodded and opened the door. Gavin was just about to walk through it when he heard his name. He turned to see Emily's husband approach, a less-than-friendly look on his face.

"A word, Lord Tamesly."

He nodded, a little wary at the man using his formal title. The rest of the family, including Diana, had referred to him as Gavin. The reference, combined with the stern expression on Michael's face, didn't boost his confidence at all.

Without a word Hughes shut the door and discreetly disappeared. Michael stepped forward and looked at Gavin for a long moment.

The man reminded him of an interrogator, able to

intimidate with just a look. However, Gavin had little patience for mental games. He appreciated the direct approach. "Is there something I can do for you, Lord Hathery? If not, I do have to meet with my cousin. He was quite insistent in his missive."

"This will take just a moment of your time." Michael took a step toward Gavin, then leaned in closely and said in a low voice, "Stay away from my wife."

Gavin jerked back, blinking with surprise. This was the last thing he'd thought he'd hear. *Zounds,* he hoped he hadn't been a rogue in the past. If that were the case, he had more to worry about than anything Michael Balcarris could do to him.

"I understand that you've lost your memory, but my wife hasn't. She is in a delicate condition right now, and her emotions are, shall I say, a bit unstable. Do not entertain any ideas of taking advantage of her."

"I would not dream of it," he said, finding the very thought of carrying on with another man's wife—his pregnant wife, for that matter—appalling.

"You do not remember the pain you put her through. I won't have her suffering at your hand again."

Now he was totally befuddled. "Pain? What the devil are you talking about?"

"You really do not know?" Michael stepped back, a confused look spreading across his face. "At first I thought this amnesia of yours might be an act . . ."

"You think I would fake something like this?" The

man had gall, he would give him that. Gavin's patience was near the expiration point. He might not remember his past, but to be accused of fakery was beyond the pale. "I assure you I am *not* pretending. I have no reason to. What would I gain by faking amnesia?"

"I do not know. I am not privy to your personal motivations. Nor do I care about them. My only concern is my family, and specifically, my wife."

"That is understandable. And admirable," Gavin added through gritted teeth. "But I can assure you I have no inclination or desire to hurt your wife. I would like to think I possess higher character than that. But if I hurt her in the past, I sincerely apologize. She is a fine woman, and not deserving of any bad behavior on my part."

Michael didn't respond right away, as if he didn't know how to take Gavin's words. Then he finally spoke. "I am to assume Colin did not tell you what happened between you and Emily before you left for India?"

A pool of dread filled Gavin's stomach. Good night, what kind of dreadful deed had he done? He swallowed. "No . . . he did not."

"Then allow me to fill in the blanks. My wife loved you. Very much."

Oh no. Gavin immediately thought the worst once again. "We had an affair?"

"I was afraid of this!" Emily suddenly stormed into

the foyer and stood between the two men. She turned and faced Michael. "I knew you didn't excuse yourself to go to the privy. Just like I knew you were going to badger poor Gavin. And all over something that happened in the past. Something that was over a long time ago!" She then faced Gavin, her countenance as fiery as her tone. "Since my husband so indelicately informed you of what happened, I shall fill in the blanks. The short story is that I fell in love with you. I was young and stupid and so desperate to have some romance in my life that I fell for the first charming gentleman who paid the least bit of attention to me."

"Oh." He didn't know whether to feel complimented or insulted.

"And you, wisely, I must add, knew this. So you did the gentlemanly thing and ended it. Because of that, I fell in love"—her voice and her stance suddenly softened—"for real."

Turning around, she touched Michael on the cheek. "You are the love of my life, darling, and you always will be. You are the most wonderful, clever, kind, and handsome man I know. You never have to worry about my old feelings for Gavin resurrecting. I put those to death a long time ago. Have I made myself clear enough to you?"

"Crystal," Michael said, his voice sheepish but his expression filled with satisfaction and love for his wife.

"Then will you leave the poor man alone, finally?"

Michael nodded, but his gaze never left hers.

Gavin had to hand it to Emily. She did a bang up job of bolstering her husband's ego all while putting him in his place. Silently he thanked her for ending the situation between he and Michael, or he might have been facing pistols at dawn.

"Now, cake has just been served," she purred." "It's filled with loads of cream. You would not deny a pregnant woman her cake now, would you?"

Michael grinned, then wiggled his eyebrows in a devilish fashion. "Absolutely not." He then reached around his wife and extended his hand toward Gavin. "Um . . . sorry about before, mate. Seems Emily isn't the only one overly emotional these days."

"I beg your pardon?" Emily sniffed. "I am *not* overly emotional! I am perfectly normal, thank you very much."

"Of course you are, dear. Anyone can see that."

"Hmmph."

Gavin grabbed Michael's hand and shook it. "No harm done. Believe me, I would react the same way if I were in your shoes."

"Then I am very glad we understand each other. I would like to put this entire unpleasantness behind us, if you are agreeable."

"We will not speak of it again."

Emily tapped her feet against the marble tiled floor. "All right, you two made up, now can we get dessert?"

"Better do as she asks," Gavin said.

"Yes, I should, or else I will pay dearly. Have a good

evening, Gavin." Michael moved to escort Emily to the dining room. As they left, Emily gave Gavin a small wave, then disappeared down the hall.

As he waited for Hughes to appear a second time with his coat, Gavin thought about what had just transpired. So that was his reason for leaving London, to spare Emily the continuing pain of unrequited love. Very selfless of him. *Too* selfless, he realized. There had to be something more to it, of that he was certain. Perhaps his encounter with Michael and Emily had been fruitful after all. Something deep inside the recesses of his mind shook loose, as if snippets of his memory were floating around, just out of his reach. He now knew that he did leave London because of a woman, but that woman wasn't Emily.

That woman was Diana.

Gavin arrived to find Percival Parringer pacing the length of his study, his boots thudding against the faded Aubusson carpet. Percival apparently hadn't heard Gavin arrive, for he continued his pacing, mumbling incoherently to himself.

Stepping away from the room, Gavin collected his thoughts, which he thought would be wise before his first encounter with his cousin. Something told him to tread carefully with this man, but he wasn't sure why. He was family, and if the Dymokes were any indication, family cared about each other and watched out for their best interests. *Zounds,* he wasn't even a blood relative of the Dymoke clan, yet he had felt their concern for him and had felt welcomed into the fold, his short conversation with Michael notwithstanding. He was very happy they had cleared up the matter before he left.

Yet he couldn't shake the feeling that Gavin's best interest was the last thing on Percival's mind.

He heard soft footsteps come up behind him. Gavin spun around to see Seamus standing in the hall. Seamus put a finger to his lips, then motioned for Gavin to follow him a few feet away from the study.

"I do not trust that lad," Seamus said when they were safely out of earshot. "There's somethin' not quite right with him."

"What do you mean?"

"When he arrived, he was beside himself when he found out you were not here. Terrorized poor Mrs. Bloomfield until she told him where you were, then demanded she get his note to you. I stepped in and delivered it for her, poor thing. She's not a bloomin' delivery boy!"

Gavin raised an eyebrow at his friend's fierce defense of their housekeeper. "I promise I will hire more help come the first of the week. What else have you noticed about Percival?"

"He has been pacing that room for the past half hour, muttering to himself. Lots of nervous energy, which usually means a lad's up to no good." He laid a hand on Gavin's arm. "Just be careful around him."

"I will. Thank you for your concern." With a nod to Seamus, he walked away and headed for the study, ready to face whatever his cousin had to say.

When he entered the room, Percival immediately stopped pacing. The shorter man looked at Gavin, a big grin splitting his face. "Gavin!" he said, his arms spreading wide. "Welcome home! I apologize for not being here when you arrived, but I was visiting a dear friend of mine in Wales."

Gavin hesitated a brief moment before accepting Percival's unexpected, and frankly insincere, welcome. He embraced his cousin loosely, then stepped back to look at him. A strand of thin black hair had become dislodged from his greased-down pate, revealing a shiny bald spot. Then he realized that the sheen from his hair wasn't hair pomade; it was perspiration.

The man was sweating. Profusely sweating.

Gavin recalled Seamus's comment about Percival's nervous energy. The doctor was right, as usual. An innocent person didn't pace or sweat, especially in the presence of a family member. Instantly he wondered what his cousin was hiding.

"Would you like a drink?" Gavin asked calmly as he strode across the room to a sideboard which held an array of decanters and glasses. He picked one up. "This is a particularly good one," he said, looking at the dark, burgundy-colored liquid. "I must say I have developed a taste for port since my return."

"You used to be a whiskey man." Percival eagerly

nodded his head when Gavin offered to pour him a glass. He slipped his hands in his pockets and started bending then straightening his knees as Gavin fixed the drink.

"What did you need to speak with me about?" Gavin asked, pouring a drink for himself, then handing one to Percival. He kept his own demeanor calm in contrast to the nervousness of his cousin. "Your note said it was of the utmost importance."

"It is." Percival quickly downed the drink, then withdrew a handkerchief from his pocket and dabbed at his forehead. "I wanted to talk to you before the rumors started. I need to set things straight."

"Rumors?" Gavin went to his desk and sat behind it. Piles of unattended paperwork cluttered his desk. He cleared a spot and set down his drink.

"About me." Percival slid into the chair across from Gavin. "You see, I am afraid that some people—your solicitor, for one—hold me in very little esteem because I wanted to have you declared dead."

"You question their reaction?" Gavin retorted, not bothering to hide his irritation. "I also find it hard to hold you in any esteem, considering you are family and you were very eager to celebrate my demise."

"That is not true!" Percival popped up from his seat. "You do not understand. It is not that I wanted to declare you dead. I am not as callous as that."

"Of course not," Gavin said dryly. "I suppose I can assume you have no interest in my title either. There must have been another reason for you to remove my portrait in the gallery."

"There was a tear in the canvas," Percival said, not looking at Gavin directly. "I am having it repaired."

"I see." What he did see was that his cousin was lying, and he didn't know why.

Percival paused for a moment, the expression on his face proving Gavin's assumption that his cousin was less than forthright true. Then he continued. "Shortly after you disappeared, I found myself in a bit of a . . . pickle, so to speak."

"What kind of a pickle?"

He sat back down and averted his gaze. "Had a bad run at the gaming tables, to tell the truth."

Gavin wasn't sure if this man knew what truth meant. "So you needed money."

Percival looked at Gavin. "Honestly, Gavin, there was absolutely no trace of you for so long. And the collectors were hassling me—"

"So if I were dead, you would inherit my money and my title. Problem solved."

"Exactly. But now you are here . . . and of course I am very happy about it . . ."

"But?" Gavin steepled his fingers together. His cousin was squirming faster than a worm on the end of a fishing line. Gavin had no intention of relieving his discomfort. That his closest relative could speak so matter-of-factly about his supposed death left a bitter taste in his mouth.

"Well, I have been able to keep them at bay for some time," Percival said. "But with your return . . . I am afraid they are barking at the door once again."

"And you have no funds with which to pay them?"

Percival shook his head.

"So instead of finding a way to obtain money to settle your debts, you spent the last seven years trying to access my birthright."

"You make me sound heartless," he said, wringing his pale hands together. "Truly, it was not like that."

"Wasn't it?" Gavin sprang up from his seat, his ire getting the best of him. "What do you expect me to say, Percival? Since I walked through that door, other than a cursory greeting—which was far from sincere—you have not uttered a single query as to my welfare. I have been gone *eight* years."

To his credit, Percival blanched.

"You have not asked me how I am getting along, or if there was anything you could assist me with. Not even a single offer to help me regain my memory. All you have talked about is your debts, your problems. Well, *dear* cousin, I have bloody problems of my own!" He swept the stacks of documents off the desk. Dozens of thin papers fluttered to the ground.

Percival slowly rose from his chair, his eyes wide as his gaze followed the trajectory of the documents hitting the floor. "Perhaps this is a bad time," he whispered.

"How very perceptive of you. But seeing as I have

allowed you your say, now I will have mine. Let me tell you what I have had to deal with since my return. I know you don't care one whit, but you are going to listen anyway."

Percival sat back down.

"I have come back to a dilapidated house, which I do not remember ever living in. I see my signature on documents I do not recognize—I do not even recognize the signature. I cannot remember even a tiny bit of my heritage, and nothing of my father or my mother." He pounded his fist on the desk. "And to top it all off, I just found out that I broke a poor woman's heart when I left London, and I think I am falling in love with a woman I barely know."

His brows knitted together in confusion, Percival said, "What?"

Gavin pulled up to a verbal stop. Where had those last words come from? Diana's image flitted across his mind, but it wasn't from supper earlier. The vision was more distant, fuzzier . . . more like a memory.

He fell into his seat and broke into a grin. "I remember," he said softly, mostly to himself.

"Gavin?" Percival leaned forward, beads of sweat still dripping down his face. "What do you remember?"

"I . . . I do not know." Just as quickly as the memory had appeared, it faded, just beyond his reach. Still, he wasn't discouraged. For the first time he remembered something, however unclear and brief the memory had been.

"If it helps any," Percival said in a small voice, "your mother died when you were young. You have never remembered her."

He looked up at his cousin, his fury suddenly abated. "That does help," he said absently, still in a semi-stupor over experiencing a memory for the first time in years. Looking down at his disheveled desk, he searched for a quill pen. "What do you need?"

"I beg your pardon?"

"How much do you need?" Gavin yanked opened a drawer and began shuffling through it. There had to be pen and paper in here somewhere. Finally he found them and pulled them out. Fortunately in his earlier fury, he hadn't knocked over the inkwell. Dipping the pen in the ink, he started scribbling on the paper. "You still haven't told me how much you need."

Percival swallowed. "You said . . . I assumed . . ."

"You assumed wrongly." Gavin scribbled an amount on the paper and signed it. "Here is my written word that I will help you out. Meet me at the bank in the morning, and we will withdraw the stated the amount. Will this at least help you get out of your pickle?"

The man accepted the paper, looked at it, and then glanced at Gavin again. "Yes," he said, folding the paper and tucking it into the pocket of his jacket.

"It is a loan," Gavin said, sternly. "I expect it to be paid back, with interest. I will have Mr. Buttons draw up an amortization schedule tomorrow, and it will be sent to you later in the day."

"Of course." Percival seemed happy enough, but Gavin couldn't help but notice the man's lack of enthusiasm. It was almost as if the amount, which had been very large, didn't satisfy him. "What made you change your mind?" he asked. "I thought you were on the verge of turning me down flat."

Gavin considered him for a moment. "You are family," he said simply, leaving it at that.

"That we are. Thank you, cousin." Percival gave him a small nod. "Now, the hour grows late, and I will leave you to enjoy the rest of your evening."

After his cousin left, Gavin was eager to seek out Seamus. The old man would be thrilled to learn about his breakthrough, and Gavin couldn't wait to tell him.

Several minutes later he located him out in the garden, smoking a pipe. The sweet, vanilla scent tickled Gavin's nose.

When he saw Gavin approach, he pulled the pipe out from between his teeth. "What is it, lad?" he said, standing up from the stone bench he'd been sitting on. "Did something happen with you and Percival?"

Gavin shook his head. "You were right, he's not to be trusted. But he is family, even if he is rather pathetic."

"What do you mean?" Alarm filled Seamus's face. "You did not give him any money, did you?"

"Of course I did. Like I said, he is family. I did not give him enough to do any damage to anyone, but at least he should have some of his creditors off his back." He gripped Seamus's shoulders. "But I do not want to talk about him." He took a deep breath. "I remembered something."

Seamus's bushy eyebrows rose. "You have?"

"Yes! It wasn't very clear, and I cannot pull the memory up now, but maybe I will be able to later. But that doesn't matter. I remembered, Seamus. I finally remembered."

"Sit down, lad." Seamus led him to the bench, then sat down beside Gavin. "Tell me exactly what you remembered."

"Like I said, it's very hazy." He closed his eyes and tried to dredge the memory up again. But it was as if it were dancing on a string, just out of his grasp.

"Who was the memory about?"

"Diana." He opened his eyes when he heard Seamus cluck his tongue. "What?"

Seamus put his arm around Gavin's shoulders. "Lad, I do not mean to discourage you, but you just saw Diana. There is nothing wrong with your short-term memory."

"But that is not what I am talking about. This memory is different. She looks different, but just as beautiful. And she is saying something, but I cannot remember what. Then . . ." he let out a sigh. "The memory is gone."

Seamus leaned forward and took a long sniff of Gavin's breath.

Gavin leaned back, confused at the doctor's behavior. "What are you doing?"

"You have been drinking, haven't you?"

"Just a little bit of port. I did not even finish the glass."

"Hmmm." Seamus stroked his salt-and-pepper beard. "The alcohol could be playing havoc with your mind, affecting your brain in some way we do not know."

"I am telling you, I had a scant half glass!" He leaped from the bench and ran his hand through his hair, grabbing at the ends in frustration. "I thought you would be happy for me."

"I am, lad." He stood and joined Gavin. "But I also do not want to give you false hope either. That would not be responsible of me as a doctor, now would it?"

Gavin looked away, deflated. "I suppose not."

Seamus squeezed Gavin's arm. "Tell you what, lad. If you have any more of these memories, write them down, and then let me know immediately. Oh, and lay off the drink for a while until we can see if it has any true effect or not. You might also think about keeping company with Diana, if that is possible."

"Keeping company with her?"

"Spend some time with her. She is the first link to your past, the only person or thing to trigger anythin' inside your mind. Perhaps bein' with her will help shake other things loose in that brain o' yours." With a grin, Seamus stood, patted Gavin on the back, and headed for the house, leaving Gavin alone in the garden.

Gavin found little comfort in his friend's words. He had hoped Seamus would agree that he'd had a breakthrough, but instead he questioned the memory as valid. And although he knew that, since Seamus was a doctor, playing the devil's advocate was often necessary, it didn't make him feel any better.

For some reason, it made him feel much worse.

But Seamus had offered some advice that he found appealing—the idea of spending more time with Diana. That was a suggestion he could get behind.

Chapter Six

Diana wanted to throttle her sister when they arrived at the Balcarris party Friday evening. Emily had been very much mistaken about the size of the event. Instead of a small, intimate gathering, it seemed half of London had shown up to Ruby Balcarris' soiree. When Diana entered the ballroom with her sister and brother-in-law and saw the impressive crush of people dancing and socializing, she felt as if she'd been tricked.

"Oh, dear," Emily said, stopping in the middle of the doorway. "Michael, what are all these people doing here?"

Michael glanced around the ballroom, appearing as perplexed as his wife. "Seems Mother underestimated the size of her guest list. Either that, or there are more than a few party crashers present."

Emily turned to Diana. "I am so sorry, Diana. I truly had no idea there would be so many people here. If I had known that, I would not have invited you."

Seeing the sincerity in her sister's eyes, Diana's ire cooled somewhat. She was glad that it had been an honest mistake, and that her sister hadn't been up to something. Patting Emily on the arm to reassure her that she wasn't too upset, she surveyed the crowded ballroom. Pressing her lips together, she fought the urge to bolt. Michael probably wouldn't mind taking her home, although she hated the idea of drawing him away from his mother's party. Still, the idea of spending the entire evening making polite small talk and feigning having a good time didn't appeal to her at all. Of course she could always order her own hack, then she wouldn't have to bother Michael. That was a better idea. Fortunately they hadn't been spotted yet. She could easily sneak away—

"Michael, darling!" Ruby appeared from the crowd, floating toward them wearing a voluminous, vibrant purple chiffon gown. Her peach-colored cheeks glowed with happiness. Ruby Balcarris was always in her element when she was playing hostess. "Hello, Emily dear." She kissed her daughter-in-law on the cheek, then reached up on tiptoe and did the same to her son. Then she turned to Diana. "I am so delighted to see you, love. I had hoped you would attend tonight. You look simply stunning."

"Thank you. You look beautiful as well." So much for her plan to leave the party undetected. It would be the height of rudeness to skip out now after being so warmly welcomed by Michael's mother. Diana sighed inwardly, bolstering herself for a long evening.

"Mother, I thought this was to be an intimate func-tion," Michael said.

"It was, darling, it was. But somehow the guest list got away from me." She gestured to the crowded crush of people behind her. "Everyone is having a delightful time, though, if I do say so. Come, join us. Emily, I had cook prepare your favorite pastries just for you."

Emily's eyes lit up for a brief moment. She looked to Diana, worry still tugging at the corners of her mouth. Diana gave her smile. "Go on, Emily. I will be fine. Look, there's Henrietta Buntington. I have not seen her ages. Now would be a good time for us to catch up."

Relief washed over her sister's features. Emily gave Diana a quick hug. "Thank you for being such a good sport," she whispered. Then she stepped back and grinned. "You will have a great time. Ruby throws the best parties, you know." She linked her arm through the crook of Michael's and led him to the dessert table. Michael glanced over his shoulder, giving Diana a helpless, but pleased, look.

She couldn't help but smile. Really, they were the

most suitable couple she knew. Michael not only knew how to handle Emily's moods and enthusiasm, he also appreciated them. To Emily's credit, she didn't seem to mind one bit that her husband's reputation was more than a bit unusual. He had always been flamboyant, almost to the point of being fey. Once he and Emily became romantically involved, he'd toned down some of his more outrageous mannerisms, but was still a dandy about town. She'd always suspected there was something else going on with him, but she never brought her suspicions up with Emily. She loved her husband to distraction, and accepted him just the way he was. They definitely brought out the best in each other.

Just as she had hoped her and William would have. What a disaster that had turned out to be.

Her smile faded, and she quickly sent the somber thought fleeing from her mind. Perhaps this was the opportunity she needed to prove to her family that she was just fine. Then they wouldn't worry about her, or pepper her with questions and suggestions about how she should live her life. She knew their concern was borne out of love, but she did find it tedious to deal with at times.

She looked for Henrietta, who seemed to have disappeared in the thick crowd. It would be nice to reconnect with her friend. They used to be very close, before Diana married William. After their marriage, Diana had insulated herself from society, not wanting to answer questions about William and their relationship.

A few years ago Henrietta had wed an earl of very wealthy means, and they had lost touch since.

She inserted herself in the crowd of people on the perimeter of the ballroom floor, and found herself instantly swept away on a wave of dancers as they exited the dance floor.

Finding it difficult to move through the crush, she decided to wait it out until the crowd thinned. Then she felt someone run into her from behind. She swirled around to face her attacker.

"A thousand pardons."

Diana looked up into the apologetic green eyes of Gavin Parringer. Of all the people to literally run into!

He looked around, shrugging his shoulders in a helpless fashion. It was the only movement he had any room to do. They stood there for a moment, getting jostled by passersby, until Gavin said, "Smashing party."

"Crushing is more like it," Diana returned. Suddenly she was shoved by a rather rude gentleman who physically demanded a wide berth by pushing everyone out of his way. Her body slammed into Gavin's.

"Oh, dear," she said, trying to step back from him. But she couldn't. There was absolutely no room. She had little left to do but look up directly into Gavin's face. When she did, they were practically nose to nose.

"Are the dowager Lady Hathery's parties always like this?" he asked, his eyes darting back and forth.

"Not usually." She detected the scent of delicious

peppermint on his breath. Her stomach tightened inside. "This one is particularly crowded."

"Apparently." His lips twitched into a smile.

They were bumped again, and despair started to seep inside her. Was she doomed to remain stuck in the crowd all night? Although she had to admit that being stuck with Gavin wasn't altogether . . . unpleasant.

As if he could read her thoughts, he said, "Do you want to get out of here?"

She nodded. "But how? We are packed in tighter than a tin of sardines."

"Let me take care of it."

Before she could utter a word of protest, he curved his arm around her shoulders and spun her around so her back pressed against his chest. Then, with his arm still protectively around her, he cleared a path through the crowd, much the same as the other gentleman had, with one exception. Gavin must have uttered a thousand "pardon me's" each time he bumped into someone.

Finally they were at the edge of the ballroom near the balcony, which led to the garden below. Diana stepped out on the stone platform and inhaled a deep breath, Gavin not far behind her.

"Thank you," she said, turning around. "I was afraid I would never be free."

"There is always an escape, Mrs. Garland," Gavin said. "Sometimes you have to search for it, other times you have to force it, but it's always there."

"That was quite profound."

"Thank you. I excel at profundity. At least I think I did." He grinned again, and once more a puzzling wave of warmth flowed through her. The sensation didn't make any sense. Why was she feeling such a strong attraction to him now? An attraction she didn't want to feel, not only for him, but for any man. She turned her face from his, lest she give away any of her confusion.

Gavin stepped to the edge of the balcony and put his hands on the wrought iron rails. "A very nice evening. Not as warm as it is in Calcutta, but nice just the same."

"That will not last for long. Summer is fast approaching."

He turned and looked at her. "Is that a problem?"

"Only if you are in the city. It gets rather pungent at times."

He nodded. "The same in Calcutta. See, the cities are not all that different, unless you count the language—"

"And the geography," she added.

"Along with the religion and politics."

"But other than that they are the same." She laughed.

He beamed. "You have a beautiful laugh." Then he spun around so she couldn't see his face. "I am sorry," he said, his back to her. "That was rather forward of me. I should not have said that."

"So then you are saying it is not true?"

He looked at her, his green eyes filled with smoky intensity. "It is absolutely true."

Diana's face heated, but not from embarrassment. She was amazed at the ease with which she could converse with Gavin. In the past she had never had a problem talking with men, but usually her interactions had been with the intent of reeling the gentleman in slowly, then cutting bait and watching him flounder. This was different—a friendly, enjoyable conversation, something she'd never have imagined she'd ever have with Gavin again. Although it did help that he remembered nothing of their former relationship.

Then reality set in. This was Gavin Parringer, for heaven's sake. They had been through this ruse before. Well, the ruse had been on her part, and of course he didn't remember it. Still, she felt guilty for enjoying his company so much.

"Did I say something wrong?" he moved toward her, concern filling his features.

She shook her head. "No. I was just remembering something." Realizing what she'd said, she brought her gloved fingertips to her forehead. "I am sorry. I should think before I open my mouth."

"Do not worry about it," he said softly. "You need not tiptoe around the subject for my benefit. I have accepted that I may never get my memory back."

She couldn't imagine having to go through life not remembering anything. Forgetting her late husband wouldn't be a bad thing, but his memory, unfortunately, was not only seared in her mind, it scarred her heart. "How do you manage?" she asked, trying to keep the terrible memories at bay.

"What do you mean?"

"How do you get through life not knowing your past? Not recognizing your friends and family?"

"I do not know," he said softly. "I just do. I have no alternative."

A lump formed in her throat. Unbidden, she stepped toward him, as if an imaginary force was somehow drawing her closer. "It must be very difficult for you."

He looked at her again. She'd never realized before what a stunning shade of green his eyes were. Or that he had an adorable cleft in the center of his chin. Then there was the dimple in his left cheek when he smiled, giving him a boyish look even though he was very much a man. Strands of silver gray were woven through the thick black hair at his temples, and creases were evident at the corner of his eyes. He had gotten older, just as they all had. But she knew it wasn't just age that had marked itself on his face. The amnesia had caused him to suffer more than she could ever fully understand.

"Tell me something, Mrs. Garland."

"Diana, if you please."

"Diana." His low voice floated over her, like harmonious notes from a rich symphony. "How well did we know each other?"

"What do you mean?" she asked, willing her face not to flush.

"Your brother is my best friend, your sister used to be in love with me." He paused. "I find it difficult to say that without sounding like a complete cad."

"I understand completely," she mumbled, feeling her cheeks heat.

"But you . . . no one has mentioned anything about you and I. Were we friends? Enemies?" With a tilt of his head, he gave her a half-smile. "Although I would hate to think we did not get along."

Goodness, he exuded charm, another quality she had forgotten he'd possessed. She looked away for a moment, trying to think of the right words without sounding positively full of herself. Which she had been, at one time. Back then she wouldn't have thought twice about playing with a man's heart, or bragging to her friends that yet one more man had fallen in love with her. Gavin included.

But this was different, and not only because she had finally grown up and left her childish ways behind. For some reason she wanted to tread lightly and carefully with Gavin. She was loathe to make him uncomfortable or to hurt his feelings, and not because she pitied him or because she was covered with the stain of guilt. If there was one thing she had learned about Gavin tonight is that he didn't deserve her pity.

He deserved her honesty.

She opened her mouth to tell him that when Emily

suddenly appeared on the balcony. "There you are!" she said, sounding slightly out of breath. "I wondered where you had gone off to." She looked at Gavin and smiled. "Good evening, Gavin. I hope you are enjoying the party."

"I am enjoying it very much," he said, looking at Diana.

For the second time that evening she blushed. Then she inwardly berated herself for it when she caught Emily's knowing look. She could keep no secrets from her sister.

"Colin is looking for you, sister dear," Emily said, moving to Diana and capturing her hand with her own.

"What does he want?" Diana asked, surprised at the force with which Emily was dragging her away from Gavin.

"Who knows, it's Colin. Probably nothing of import, but still, he asked that I find you." When they reached the edge of the ballroom, Emily released her hand. "He is on the other side of the room."

Diana looked at the crowded ballroom, not in any hurry to get stuck in there again. "I am sure whatever it is can wait," she said, stepping backward.

"No, it cannot!"

Raising an eyebrow at Emily's forceful tone, she faced her sister. "You just said you had no idea what he wanted."

"I know what I said," Emily responded, looking more than a bit vexed. "But what I *meant* was that he would not have asked me to get you if it was not important."

"Come again?"

"Just go see him!" Emily said, shoving Diana into the room. Immediately she was swallowed up by the crowd. When she turned around, all she could see were the people huddling around her.

Gavin had disappeared.

"Not very subtle, are you?"

Emily patted the back of her chignon, which was impressively coiled at the nape of her neck and decorated with white pearls. "I do not know what you mean."

Gavin smirked. "You are not a very good liar either."

"Bother," she said, then huffed. "Of course I am not a good liar. And you are right, I have never been very good at subtlety. But I needed to speak to you privately, and using my brother as an excuse was the only thing I could think of."

Gavin suspected Colin had been used as an excuse many times in the past by Emily in order to achieve what she wanted. And obviously she wanted something from him. "Does your husband know you're out here?"

"No, and if we speak quickly he won't."

He blanched. "I thought we had straightened all that out."

"We have, but there's no need to rub his nose in it.

Listen, I am not here to talk about my husband. I am here to talk about Diana."

"I was afraid of that."

"And just what is that supposed to mean?"

"Nothing." He gave a wave of his hand. "Suffice to say that I was forewarned about your matchmaking proclivities."

"By my sister?"

"No, by Clarissa."

"Well that little imp." Emily put her hands on her hips, her swollen belly jutting impressively outward. "My brother needs to have a talk with that girl."

"He knows," Gavin said. He craned his neck to peek around Emily's very full figure. The last thing he wanted was another messy encounter with Michael. Their last conversation had ended on a good note, and he didn't want to tempt fate. "If you are here to match me with your sister—"

"Now if you will just listen for a moment—"

"Then I will save you the trouble, because I am not interested."

"That is the biggest lie in the history of lying," she said, clearly insulted.

"No, it is not."

Emily's face turned bright red. "How can you possibly say that? Do you not understand—every man that has ever taken a breath has been besotted by my sister. Even you!"

"Me?" Gavin's eyes grew wide at receiving this new piece of the puzzle of his past.

"Yes, you. Although you clearly do not remember it." She tilted up her chin. "You, Gavin Parringer, were in love with my sister. So desperately in love, you left India to escape her."

Gavin leaned against the balcony for support. "I thought you said *you* were in love with me."

"I was."

"So both of you were in love with me?"

Emily rolled her eyes. "Gavin, do not be daft. You loved her. I loved you. You did not love me, and Diana did not love you. Diana became engaged to William Garland, and then you left the country. It is as simple as that."

He rubbed his temples. "There is nothing simple about that scenario."

"Well, I suppose not. But it is what it is . . . er, what it was." She frowned. "Now you are making me confused."

Gavin decided right there and then that Michael had to be a saint for dealing with Emily, or an extremely intelligent man to be able to discern her ping-pong style of conversation. He felt a headache coming on straightaway.

"Look, all I want you to do is ask her to dance," Emily said, finally getting to the point.

"Dance?" he asked, still trying to wrap his head

around the romantic triangle he'd had no idea he'd been a part of. But it did explain why the one memory he had would be of Diana. And why he left England. It wasn't just to spare Emily's feelings, but to spare his own. That premise he could swallow.

"Gavin? Are you even listening to me?" Emily touched him on the arm.

"What? Yes, yes, of course I am. You want me to ask her to dance."

"Just one dance."

"And I have one question. Why? You just said she never had any feelings for me." A sudden sharpness penetrated his heart at the sound of the words. The sensation hurt far worse than wounded pride.

"Because she's vulnerable," Emily said. "Since William died, she has done little more than spend time alone at home. She rarely attends parties and she definitely does not entertain anymore."

Gavin bit the inside of his lip. It saddened him to think of her being alone. "I still do not understand why you thought of me. I figured I would be the last person you would want around your sister."

"At one time that was true, but not now. Her feelings are still tender, Gavin. She has lost the ability to open up to someone again. I trust that you won't trample on her emotions, or play her for a fool."

"And why do you trust me so much, Emily? You have not seen me in eight years. I am not the man I used to be."

"There is where you are wrong, Gavin. Just because you do not remember who you were does not mean you aren't still the same person." She leaned forward, smiling. "Besides, I would have never fallen in love with a cad."

He chuckled at that. "Well then, I'll take that as a high compliment."

"You should. I do not give them freely. Now, will you ask Diana to dance? Or must she spend the rest of the evening avoiding several dodgy characters who have already taken an interest in her?"

He didn't like the sound of that at all. "Yes," he said with a nod. "I will ask her to dance."

"Splendid!" She clapped her gloved hands together, then let out a gasp and clutched her side.

"Emily?" He moved toward her, alarmed.

"I am all right," she muttered, rubbing her side. "The baby has good, strong legs. Every once in a while she catches me off guard."

"She?"

"Or he. I usually go back and forth. I hate calling my baby an it."

"Completely understandable."

Her eyes suddenly widened. "There he goes again. Here, can you feel that?"

Before he could say—or do—anything, Emily had snatched his hand and put it on her belly. Underneath his palm he could feel the baby's movement. He couldn't help but smile, all while furtively hoping

Michael wouldn't choose that moment to walk out on the balcony.

Emily, on the other hand, didn't seem a bit worried. "I told you he was strong."

After feeling one more kick, Gavin prudently removed his hand. "You are right. He—or she—definitely has some muscles."

"Michael Andrew was like that." She sighed, patted her belly, then let her arm fall to her side. "As much as I enjoy being pregnant, I will be glad when this baby is finally born."

"Are you close to your time?"

She shook her head. "No. I do not expect him to come for another couple of months. But enough about me. Now, run along and find Diana before the orchestra takes a break."

"Only if you are sure—"

"I am sure! Honestly, Gavin, I do not remember you being this argumentative."

"And I do not remember you being this tenacious."

"Then you really have forgotten everything, because if there is one thing I have been called many a time, it is tenacious. Or was that tedious? Well, anyway, you have your mission, so off you go." She shooed him away.

With a grin, he turned and headed for the ballroom, marveling at Emily's powers of persuasion and her honest concern for her sister. If he were honest with himself, he would have to admit that he found the idea of dancing with Diana very appealing. Although he never would have asked her if Emily hadn't urged him to.

He wouldn't have had the courage.

Suddenly he stopped and turned around, compelled to tell her the truth. "You were right, Emily. I lied to you before."

"About what?" she asked.

"About not being interested in Diana." He glanced down at his polished shoes, then looked back at her. "My mind might have forgotten about her . . . but my heart definitely remembers."

Chapter Seven

Diana was beginning to wish she'd never agreed to come to this party. Since her sister had pulled her away from Gavin, she had yet to find Colin, but had been approached by no less than eight single gentlemen asking her to dance. When she refused, they asked permission to call. When she said she was too busy, they questioned her about her activities. She had to be downright rude to a couple of men who wouldn't leave her alone, and she had yet to have a single glass of lemonade to cool her parched throat. All in all it was turning out to be a dreadful evening.

Except for the time she spent with Gavin.

If it weren't for Emily, she would still be talking to him. He didn't seem eager to return to the party once they were on the balcony. Not that she blamed him.

Since his return the gossipy tongues of genteel society had been wagging endlessly, discussing poor Lord Tamesly's unfortunate state. She had to admire him for showing up at all.

But on the other hand, she wasn't too surprised by his appearance at the party tonight. He had never been the type of man to care about what others thought of him, which was one reason why he had pursued her with such reckless, and some might say embarrassing, abandon. He had never let someone else's opinion keep him from staying the course. She couldn't admit to having the same kind of freedom, and she envied him for it.

Yet thinking about Gavin was pointless, considering she was stuck here at this overblown party, and probably wouldn't see him for the rest of the night. He might have been wise enough to pack it in and leave, something she longed to do. Forgetting about her brother, she moved to the front of the house. She would call her own hack to take her back home.

Suddenly a man stepped in front of her, blocking her path. She looked up at the gentleman.

"So lovely to see you here tonight, Mrs. Garland."

Disappointment threaded through her. She should have known Percival Parringer would be here tonight. Although she'd never admitted it to anyone, Percival had been one of the reasons she rarely went out anymore. She had hoped with this being a family party, he wouldn't be here.

She should have known better. The man had been crashing events for the last decade.

Dressed in an ill-fitting burgundy and black paisley waistcoat, loosely tied cravat, and trousers so tight-fitting she thought they would burst the seams, he took a step back to gauge her own appearance. A creepy sensation spilled over her as he took his time with his perusal of her. By the time he finished looking her up and down, she felt she had been visually stripped of everything. At the last party she attended, Percival hadn't hidden his blatant desire to be with her, even if his behavior bordered on the verge of impropriety.

"You look positively stunning," he said in a low, slightly slurred voice.

She fought the urge to make a face at the smell of whisky on his breath. If any other man had said those words, they would have been meant as a compliment. Coming from Percival, they were only lewd.

He leaned forward and breathed in deeply. "And you smell as if you would love to be ravished."

Ugh, he was so distasteful, not to mention insulting. She knew from experience that to engage him was to encourage him, so she didn't respond to his oily words. Instead, she desperately searched the crowded room, wishing she could find her brother or Michael. Someone who could dispense with this man a lot more easily and quickly than she could. Unfortunately, neither of them were in sight.

"Would you care to dance?" he said, sliding closer to her, until they were inches away from each other.

Repulsed, she took a step back. "I am afraid I must say no, Mr. Parringer. I was just leaving the party."

"So early? The night has barely begun."

She mashed her lips tightly together before saying, "That may be so, however for me, the evening has ended."

He grasped her forearm, gripping it tightly, and in such a way that no one could see him. "Just one quick dance, that is all I want. Just . . . one . . . dance."

Diana tried to twist out of his grip, but she couldn't. "You are hurting me," she whispered, not wanting to make a scene.

"And you are being a snob." He sneered at her. "I have been watching you. Turning down men left and right, making them feel as if they are not good enough for you." His fingers dug deeper into her arm. "Do you think the same thing about me? Am I not good enough for you?"

"Stop it," she said, her breath catching in her throat. "Let me go."

"Never."

To Gavin's dismay, it was proving very difficult for him to find Diana. He had spent at least ten minutes just navigating through the perimeter of the ballroom. He had even spied Colin, but Diana was nowhere in sight. Still, he pressed on, not so much out of loyalty to keeping his word to Emily, but because he couldn't wait to hold Diana in his arms.

Something told him that embracing her would be like embracing a little piece of heaven.

Finally, he saw her across the room. A small smile playing on his lips, he moved to make his way to her when a woman stepped directly in front of him.

"Hello there!" She threw her arms around him and hugged him to her ample bosom.

As politely as he could he disentangled himself from her grasp. "I am sorry, do I know you?" he asked, not possessing the time or inclination to play guessing games with her.

"I do not think so, but we can fix that little oversight very quickly." She grinned, and he had to admit she was attractive, with lovely blue eyes and strawberry-blond hair. They seemed to be about the same age. Her black eyelashes fluttered as she looked him up and down. "My goodness, you are quite the fit man, aren't you?"

"Beg your pardon?"

"Come now. Do not be shy." She leaned forward and whispered, "My husband is not here tonight."

He wasn't sure what her husband's absence had to do with him, until he felt her grab his backside, the movement hidden by the surrounding crowd. He jumped and tried to shift away from her grasp.

"Let us have a dance, shall we?" she asked, flashing her lashes at him again.

"I apologize," he said, dodging her groping hand again, "but I have already promised another woman the next dance."

Her blue eyes narrowed with ire. "Tell her you cannot."

Somehow he had to escape this woman before she tackled him to the dance floor. Either she was desperate or daft. He suspected both.

Then he looked across the room at Diana again. From the expression on her face her conversation with Percival had taken a bad turn. Propelling himself away from the woman, he said, "If you will excuse me, I must take my leave." Disengaging from her, he rushed through the mass of people and toward Diana, whose problems with Percival seemed to have escalated, if the look on her face was any indication.

He had to reach her, and soon.

Diana didn't know what to do. Percival's grip grew tighter on her arm, and his expression turned stormy. Frantically she tried to escape his hold, but it was no use.

"Now . . . about that dance," he sneered.

"Is there a problem here?"

Diana turned her head and nearly cried with relief when she saw Gavin.

Percival immediately released her, then stepped to the side as if nothing was amiss. "No, Gavin," he said, straightening his cravat. "Everything is fine here. We were just about to have a dance." He looked at Diana with half-squinted eyes. "Weren't we, Mrs. Garland."

Before Diana could speak Gavin interjected. "I am sorry, that is not possible."

"Oh?" Percival's gaze narrowed. "And why is that?"

"Because she had already promised this dance to me."

Surprised, she looked up at Gavin, who instantly met her querying gaze. His eyes told her all she needed to know. "Oh, yes, my lord. I apologize, I had completely forgotten."

"Which is why I am here to remind you." He crooked his arm in her direction and looked at Percival, his expression filled with challenge, his features unflinching. Obviously he had not believed his cousin's story that everything was as innocent as it seemed.

Percival frowned, meeting Gavin's gaze for a long moment. Then he backed away from them both. But Diana noticed his cheek twitch when she slid her arm inside the crook of Gavin's. Percival looked directly at her, his displeasure evident in his cold hard stare. He bowed stiffly. "Perhaps next time, Mrs. Garland." He paused, waiting for her to respond.

Diana didn't say a word.

Clearly insulted by her lack of response, he scowled at her, then at Gavin, before turning away.

Gavin dropped his arm and faced her, genuine concern etched in his features. "Diana, are you all right?"

"Y-yes," she said, suddenly feeling very, very cold.

"You are shaking," he said quietly, his brows knitting together. "Blast my cousin. What did he do to you?"

"Nothing," she whispered, not wanting to drag Gavin into her problems. He had enough to worry about. She looked up at him, forcing her body to keep still. "Really, I am fine. Mr. Parringer asked me to dance, and I did not feel like it at the moment. I do not think he liked my answer. That is all."

"And I think it is more than that." He glanced in the direction Percival disappeared in, then looked back at Diana. "I do not like the way he was looking at you."

She didn't answer him. Instead, she looked away.

Gavin let out a breath. "All right. I will not pry. Just know that if you need me to take care of that bloke, I will be more than happy to. Actually, I would be *very* happy to. He might be part of my family, but that does not mean he can disrespect you and get away with it."

Diana couldn't help but smile at Gavin's gallantry. "I can handle him," she responded, despite doubting her words even as she said them. "But I do appreciate your intervention."

"You are more than welcome."

They stood there for a few moments, perched at the edge of the ballroom, still surrounded by jovial partygoers. The orchestra started a new tune, a slow, romantic-sounding melody. Gavin looked around for a moment, then took in a deep breath, as if he were steeling himself for something.

"So . . ." he said, sounding less confident than he had a minute ago. "Um, would you like to dance?"

His sudden uncertainty charmed her. Despite herself, she answered, "I suppose we should, considering we just told your cousin that I promised to dance with you."

Gavin nodded. "You would not want him to think you a liar, would you?"

She didn't care one whit what Percival Parringer thought of her. "Absolutely not."

He offered his arm again. "Shall we?"

Her arm easily slid into his, as if it had always belonged there. With ease and grace he led her onto the dance floor and put his hand on her waist, all in one smooth motion. She loved how his large palm easily spanned her back. In the matter of an evening he had managed to almost completely undo her vow to stay away from men. Then she reminded herself that she had promised to help him regain his memory. This dance was not a romantic venture, but a practical one.

At least that is how she rationalized it.

From the first note of the song, he led her flawlessly around the dance floor. He had always been a gifted dancer. "You have not lost your dancing ability, I see," she remarked.

"Apparently not. I guess there are some things you

never forget." He smiled. "Although I will admit that phrase has taken on a whole new meaning as of late."

She returned his smile, every ounce of tension now drained from her. "I think it is wonderful that you have a sense of humor about the situation."

His grin grew wider. He had positively perfect teeth. "I have to, or I would be certifiable. Come to think of it, some doctors might consider me as such."

"Then they would be wrong," she said.

They danced in silence for a moment, and Diana marveled at how comfortable she felt in his arms. He was a strong, lean man, who moved with near-perfect grace. William had been far less skilled on the dance floor. She frowned. Why did he always have to intrude on her thoughts?

"Is there something wrong?"

"No," she said, then immediately felt guilty for lying. What was it about Gavin that made her feel like she had to be completely honest with him? Maybe because she had always been less than honest with him in the past. Now she had a chance to rectify that. "I know it is bad form of me, but I was thinking about my husband . . . my late husband, that is."

"William?"

"Yes."

His gaze softened. "You must have loved him very much."

She didn't respond. Instead she looked away.

"I am sure you two had a wonderful relationship."

"We had our moments." And they had, early on during their courtship and the first six months of their marriage.

"I am glad to hear that. And while we are being completely honest . . ." He swirled her around in a seamless move, her slippers nearly lifting off the ground. "I have something to tell you."

"You were thinking about your husband too?" she asked with a wink, trying to interject some levity into the conversation and take it off of William.

"Very funny." He grinned for a brief moment, then grew serious. "No, actually I wanted to tell you about my conversation with Emily."

Diana's good humor faded a little at his change in mood. "What did she say?"

"Well, she did a more thorough job of explaining why I left England."

Her heart sank to her knees. "She did?"

"Yes, she did. Seems she was in love with me, and I was in love with someone else. Someone who didn't love me back."

Awkward didn't begin to describe how Diana felt. "Gavin . . . I . . . I do not know what to say. I am so sorry."

He looked genuinely surprised. "Why are you apologizing?"

She quirked a brow. "Should I not?"

"Diana, it is not your fault you did not love me."

"But it is my fault you left!"

"Did Emily forget the part of the story where you held a gun on me and forced me to flee the country?"

"No, but—"

"Then I left on my own accord."

"But if you had not left, then you would not have gotten amnesia . . ." She looked up at him, stricken. "Dear Lord, this is all my fault."

The song ended, and so did the dance. But Gavin apparently wasn't ready to end the conversation. He grabbed her hand and led her off the dance floor.

"Where are we going?" she asked as she tried to keep up with his long strides.

"Somewhere quiet," he said over his shoulder.

"Why?"

"We need to talk."

Chapter Eight

There were other guests on the balcony, so Gavin headed down the stone steps to the garden. Torches dancing with flickering light had been strategically placed throughout the fragrant patch of flowering greenery. Gavin led Diana to an elaborately carved wooden bench near a group of rose bushes. There were several people milling in the garden, but here they had a modicum of seclusion.

Diana's chest heaved, and not only from the exertion of dashing into the garden. Her hand tingled in Gavin's grasp, one she was acutely aware that he still held firm. He seemed not to notice as they sat down. Turning, he faced her.

"My accident is *not* your fault," he said. "I chose to leave."

"Yes, but I was the reason."

He smirked. "I am sorry to inform you, but the world does not revolve around Diana Garland."

She didn't appreciate his condescending tone. "I know that. But . . ." She paused. "I used to think that it did." She pulled her hand from his and stood. "I am ashamed when I think of how self-centered I used to be."

"But you are not like that anymore."

"Really?" She let out bitter laugh and turned around, facing him. "How do you know? You said you do not remember me . . . and I am starting to think that is a good thing."

"I do not." He rose from the bench. "Diana, there are so many pieces missing from my life. I cannot remember my parents or my friends. I have had to re-learn the layout of my own house. I am still trying to figure out who I can trust and who I need to be wary of. But all that pales in comparison to finding out that I loved someone, and loved them so much I gave up everything because I could not be with her. That part hurts the most."

"I do not understand."

He bent his knees a bit so he could look her straight in the eye. "I feel deep down that I have missed out on something incredibly special. And even though it did not work out the way I wanted it to, I would give anything to remember that feeling again. To remember what it was like to be that much in love."

Diana's heart lodged in her throat. Truly, she'd had no idea how passionate Gavin Parringer had been. And still was. That he mourned an unrequited love, not because he couldn't have it, but because he couldn't remember experiencing it at all, was incredible. Her heart went out to him. "Do you think you will ever get your memories back?"

He straightened, then shrugged. "I do not know. I hope so. I had a bit of a breakthrough earlier this week."

She clasped her gloved hands together, genuinely happy for him. "Gavin, that is wonderful! That is a good sign, is it not?"

"I thought so. Then I told Seamus about it, and he thought I might be experiencing a more recent memory rather than one from the past. The more I think about it, the more he may be right. Especially since I have not had any recurrences since."

"But could Seamus be wrong? Maybe it was a long-ago memory like you initially thought. What was it about?"

In the dim lighting of the garden, Gavin's face took on an odd expression. Then she realized what it was—he was blushing. He looked away for a moment, clearly discomfited.

"I am sorry," she said, taking a step back from him. "I should not had been so nosy. Really, it is not any of my business."

He turned and looked at her. "Actually, it is." Their

gazes locked, and she trembled at the expression on his face. "Diana, my memory . . . was of you."

The following morning, Gavin walked into his study and stared at the mess of papers strewn across his desk. He had haphazardly picked them up the other day after his display of temper in front of Percival and hadn't looked at them since. But he knew he'd put off the unpleasant task for long enough. It was time to tackle his long-neglected paperwork.

As he sat down behind his desk—quite a nice piece of furniture, he realized—his thoughts were far from business matters and squarely on Diana. What kind of addlebrain was he, telling her about his memory? He hadn't actually described it to her, but informing her that she had been the focus of it wasn't one of his brightest moves. First off, she had looked quite shocked. Secondly, he'd had little chance to explain himself, what with her friend Henrietta showing up at the worst possible time and dragging her back into the party, a party he hadn't really wanted to attend in the first place. From the morose look on her face when he had bumped into her, she didn't look like she wanted to be there either.

He'd spent the night dreaming about her, not surprisingly. But these dreams were clearly recent ones, as he relived their dance together—the perfect way she fit into his arms, the lavender scent of her hair, the sparkle in her eyes as they danced and talked. By the end of the night he knew exactly why he'd fallen in love with her eight years ago, and blast if he weren't dangling on the precipice of falling in love with her again.

But that would be a mistake. A huge mistake—one he'd already made. Whatever the reasons were—and she was entitled to them—she found him ill-suited for her at the time. He seriously doubted she would find him suitable now, especially since he had very little to offer. The last thing he needed was to deal with unrequited love again. He was certain the first go round had been bad enough.

But while he was doing a bang up job of convincing his mind that he shouldn't give Diana a second thought, his heart stubbornly refused to listen.

"I'm doomed," he mumbled.

"What was that, my lord?"

Gavin looked up to see Cecil Buttons walk into the room. He lifted a brow in surprise.

"I hope you don't mind, but I asked Mrs. Bloomfield to let me in. I assumed you would be asleep after your night at the Balcarris fete."

"I came home early," Gavin said, turning his attention to his papers. "I have been up since seven thirty."

"Ah. Well, they say the early riser gets the worm."

"I will have to take your word for it." Gavin glanced up at him. "What are you doing here, Mr. Buttons? It is a Saturday, after all. I would think you would be enjoying a day of leisure."

"I have never been one for leisure, my lord. I had hoped to tackle some of the paperwork on your desk for you."

Gavin looked up, surprised. "You were planning to work on my personal papers without conferring with me?"

Buttons tugged at his cravat. "Only the tedious ones. Actually, it was my habit to come in on a Saturday and open your correspondence in your absence. I guess I should have consulted you on the matter first. I apologize for overstepping my bounds."

"No harm done. You have taken excellent care of my estate."

"I only wish I could have done more, my lord."

"Nonsense, you have gone above and beyond in protecting my interests. I do thank you for your diligence, and appreciate everything you have done for me. I assure you, you will be paid for your time and effort."

"Thank you, my lord."

"But consider this official notice that I am relieving you of your duties as of this morning. Go out and have some fun. Take a ride in Hyde Park. It is such a lovely day for one."

"My lord?" Buttons appeared shocked.

"What is it?"

"You told me to ride in Hyde Park."

"So?"

"Do you *remember* Hyde Park?"

Gavin hesitated. He had no idea where the suggestion came from. His mind tried to conjure up an image of the park, but he couldn't. "I do not seem to."

"But you must. Everyone goes riding in Hyde Park—it was the perfect suggestion to make."

Frowning, Gavin said, "Must have been a lucky guess. Or I passed the park sometime last week."

"Perhaps." He hesitated for a moment, then said, "Are you sure you do not need my help? I could catch you up to speed on what has been going on during your absence."

"Mr. Buttons, I think I can figure things out." Gavin wondered if the man had always been so consumed with work.

"Right, then, I will take my leave. But do not hesitate—"

"To send for you if I need your help."

Buttons smiled. "Have a pleasant afternoon, my lord."

"You do the same," Gavin replied.

Gavin watched the portly solicitor exit the room, thinking how fortunate he was to have such a diligent employee. He glanced down at his desk. Where to start? Before long he was mired in organizing papers, setting them into stacks, and looking at ledgers. Buttons had kept meticulous records and had taken care of as much of the daily operations of the estates and holdings as he could, but it was obvious his hands had been tied in certain situations. Fortunately, it wouldn't take Gavin long to sort things out.

After several hours he leaned back in his chair and rubbed his eyes. The numbers were swimming in his head.

"Ready to call it a day?" Seamus walked into the study, and Gavin was grateful to see him.

"Absolutely. I have had enough of sorting eight years of records."

"Looks like you have made some headway," Seamus said, his gaze scanning the neat piles on Gavin's desk.

"A fair amount. However, there is much more to do." He leaned forward in his chair. Then he sighed. "But I am not going to fret about it anymore today. I've got a headache from all of this."

"Good to hear. Not about the headache of course, but that you have decided to pack it in. You need to indulge in some leisurely activities, or you will turn into a dull man. Why don't you join me at the theater this evening?"

"Theater?"

"Plays. Dramas. Actors gettin' on stage and puttin' together a story or a show."

Gavin couldn't remember going to a play. There hadn't been any in Calcutta.

"Tonight the acting troupe is performing a new rendition of an old work by Shakespeare. Should be quite enjoyable."

Gavin nodded, then looked at Seamus more carefully. "Is that a new waistcoat?"

"Indeed." He turned around so Gavin could get a complete view. "I had it made last week."

"It looks custom."

"It is."

Gavin grinned. "I had no idea there was a hidden fashion plate beneath your gruff exterior, Seamus."

"I did not either, lad. I must say I have been enjoying my time here in London. I had never fully appreciated the city until now."

"Why not?"

"I spent my youth growing up in Aberdeen, then my schooling here in England. I was so focused on my studies I never took the time to enjoy life." He frowned. "I do have some regrets."

Gavin waited for Seamus to continue, but the man didn't seem eager to elaborate. Respecting his privacy, Gavin said, "I think the theater sounds like a splendid idea. Just let me get changed."

"Aye, you do that. We should probably get a bite to eat while we are out. If you are so inclined, that is." He went to Gavin and put an arm around his shoulder. "I think it will do you good to get out on the town and see more of London. Maybe you will see something that will jog your memory."

"Maybe." Gavin thought about telling Seamus about mentioning Hyde Park to Buttons, but he held back. No doubt Seamus would dismiss it as coincidence, just as

Gavin had. No reason to speak about it. Instead he ran upstairs and readied himself for an evening out.

"Gavin! We're goin' to be late, lad. Get a move on!"

Hearing Seamus calling from downstairs, he dragged a comb through his hair, tied his cravat, and reached for his evening jacket. He put everything else out of his mind, fully intending to enjoy an evening at the theater.

Chapter Nine

"Thank you so much, darling, for accompanying me tonight." Elizabeth Dymoke leaned over and whispered into Diana's ear. "Poor Ruby had to cancel. Last night's bash completely wiped her out."

Diana smiled and patted her mother's hand. "My pleasure, Mama. I haven't been to the theater in ages."

"Keep your expectations low, dear," Elizabeth replied. "Word is that this play is dreadful."

"Then why did we come?"

"Your brother has season tickets, and he bought this box a couple years ago. He and Lily have not been to the theater in months, and I hate to see it go to waste. Oh, the curtain is going up. Shh."

The lights in the theater house dimmed, and the actors took their positions on stage. From the box seat-ing in the side balcony area, Diana squinted as she tried to see the actors. Ten minutes into the play she didn't bother anymore. Her mother had been right—the play was positively horrific.

A shuffling movement to her right caught her attention, and in the shadowy light of the theater house she saw two men slipping into the box seats beside her. A large space separated them, but she could instantly tell that one of the men was Gavin. Her pulse jumped a little at the sight of him. What was he doing here?

She leaned forward in the box, surreptitiously watching him. Suddenly he looked to the side and spotted her. He lifted his hand in the barest of waves as he sat down. She gave him a tiny wave back, then settled back in her seat. A smile played on her lips, and the play was instantly forgotten. All she could think about was Gavin.

Her mind wandered back to the party the night before, when he had admitted that his one memory had been of her. She'd been flattered, and quite pleased. But later on when she returned home, she'd spent the rest of the night tossing and turning as she tried to sort out her unexpected feelings. Confusion ruled her thoughts. She couldn't deny that she felt something for Gavin, but she couldn't pinpoint what it was. Friendship? There already seemed to be a growing camaraderie between them, and she definitely admired how he had handled the adversity he'd experienced. She could easily visualize them becoming good friends.

Yet she felt something else was blooming deep inside her, an emotion that went beyond admiration and friendship. She couldn't define it, and part of her didn't want to, for she was afraid of her true feelings for Gavin, which seemed to be multiplying at an inexplicable and alarming rate. The last thing she wanted was to have romantic feelings about anyone.

"Diana?"

She turned and looked at her mother in the suddenly bright theater. She'd been so lost in her musings, she hadn't even noticed the curtain had lowered for intermission. The play was half over and she hadn't even realized it.

"I need a bit of a stretch, love," her mother said, rising from her seat. She straightened the voluminous skirts of her aubergine-colored evening dress, then adjusted her stylish chapeau. "Would you care to join me?"

Diana shook her head. "No. I will stay here."

Elizabeth nodded, then left the box seat for the lobby of the theater, no doubt to mix and mingle with a few of her friends. Having had her fill of socializing the night before, Diana sat back in her seat and watched the crowd of people below her with interest.

"Hello, Diana."

She turned to see Gavin standing at the edge of the box seat, a program in his hand. With a smile she said, "Good evening, Gavin."

"Lovely play."

She marveled that he said the words with a straight face. Then she caught the glint in his eye and she laughed. "Oh yes, the best one thus far."

"Then I must say, I am glad I missed the season."

His remark caused her to laugh. "You should be. I wish I could say the same." She saw he still remained on the outside of the boxed area, as if waiting for her to invite him in. She didn't want to disappoint him. "Would you like to sit down?" She motioned to the seat next to her.

"I would not want to intrude." But his tone sounded like he wanted to intrude, very much so.

Really, what would it hurt if he sat down for a few moments? Besides, she also found that she wanted the company. "Mother will not be back for a while. I am sure she's catching up on the latest gossip that she might have missed at the party last night." She gestured to the plush chair again, not willing to turn him away. "Please, I insist."

Gavin strode in and sat down. Diana was acutely aware of him and his close proximity. He smelled of soap and a fresh, musky-scented cologne, and he looked far more handsome than was possibly legal in his evening suit.

Despite the terrible entertainment, the evening had taken a definite upturn.

"We seem to be running into each other quite a bit lately," Gavin said, inwardly questioning the wisdom of sitting so close to Diana, especially when she looked absolutely stunning tonight. "I hope I have not caused a problem."

She looked genuinely surprised. "Why would you say that?"

"I just thought . . . well, considering our past and everything . . ." He halted his words. He sounded like a bloody idiot. Best to be straightforward and not beat around any bushes. They were both adults; there was no reason why they couldn't handle what had happened in the past—even though he wasn't sure exactly what had happened, or if he had done anything insanely humiliating to either him or her.

He turned in the chair and faced her straight on. "I never want to make you feel uncomfortable, Diana. So if my presence brings back any bad memories for you, or if you would rather I just go away—"

Her finger went to his lips. "I am not uncomfortable, Gavin."

His eyebrows shot up. Apparently she wasn't, since she felt at ease with her finger on his mouth in a very public theater. Granted, there was no one nearby that saw them, but all someone had to do was look up with their little opera glasses and they would get an interesting eyeful, indeed.

"And," she added, slowly moving her hand away and looking more than a little shocked at the gesture she had just made, "I do not want you to go. In fact,

I am glad you are here." The uncertainty left her eyes. Then she smiled.

And his heart melted.

She truly had no idea the effect she had on him, and he knew he was playing with fire. She considered them friends, and he should be satisfied with that. Really, friends were the only thing they could be, the only thing that made logical sense.

But blast if he wanted much, much more than friendship. And double blast that he would never have it.

"So, who are you here with?" she asked, apparently, and fortunately, blissfully ignorant of the turmoil churning inside him. If she knew what he was really thinking and feeling she would have fled in an instant, and he wouldn't have blamed her at all.

"Seamus. He is a good friend of mine. I mentioned him at dinner the other night. He's the doctor who took care of me in Calcutta."

"Funny, his name doesn't sound Indian."

"He is not. He is a Scot, but he lived in India for twenty years. A long story, but he went there as a personal physician to the governor, then ended up working in a clinic in one of the poorest areas of the city."

"And you met when he found you on the docks."

"Yes. But I don't remember that at all. I just know what Seamus told me. He said when he found me I had been nearly beaten to death. My head especially took quite a few blows. When I regained consciousness,

I could not tell him anything. I had no idea who I was or even my name. He could tell from my accent that I was from London, but other than that, there were no clues to my identity. Whoever had attacked me had stolen everything—my clothes, wallet, money—anything I had of value."

Her rosebud mouth formed an O-shape. "Oh, how dreadful."

"It was. That I do remember. The pain of waking up, of not knowing anything about who I was or how I had gotten there. It took a long time for me to heal but I did, with Seamus's expert care. When I was able to function, I felt like I owed him everything, but I had nothing to give him. I offered to help him in the clinic, and he agreed. I learned a lot working with him, although I do not think my debt to him will ever be repaid. He saved my life." When he looked at Diana, he was stunned to see the sadness in her eyes. "I am sorry," he said, wishing he'd kept his mouth shut. "I did not mean to upset you. I should not have rambled on like that."

"Do not be sorry. I am glad you told me what happened to you. I am just so sorry that you had to go through that."

"I am a stronger person for it."

"I can tell."

He couldn't help but smile at the compliment. She had an amazing gift of making him feel like the most special man on Earth, and he adored feeling that way.

The house lights blinked, signaling the end of intermission. "I should be getting back to my seat. The play is about to start."

"We would not want to miss a minute of it, would we?" She smiled. "I am sorry, that was not very nice of me."

"Perhaps not." He grinned. "But it was extremely accurate." He moved to get up, but she put her hand on his arm.

"Stay a little longer."

He could barely hear the words, but he didn't miss the way she said them. Or the darkening of her crystalline blue eyes, eyes that seemed to reach deep inside his soul. At that moment he knew he wouldn't refuse her anything.

To his great surprise, he saw her move her hand toward his, then entwine their fingers together. He felt her hand tremble as their gazed melded.

Did friends hold hands? Perhaps this was another English custom he had forgotten, but for some reason he didn't think so. If anything, he thought that for her to initiate such contact was not only uncharacteristic, but very bold as well. "Diana," he murmured, unable to resist squeezing the delicate hand encased in smooth, peachy-pink satin. "What are you doing? What are *we* doing?"

"I do not know," she said, looking at him through lowered lashes, her shy response in direct contrast to the self-assured gesture. "I . . . I just had to touch you." She returned his squeeze, then looked up at him with such open honesty that he felt his breath shoot right out of him.

When he could finally speak, he said, "I am glad you did."

"Do . . . do you want me to let go?"

Did he want her to let go? Never! "No," he said simply, afraid if he added any more of his amorous thoughts to her answer she would drop his hand like a hot poker.

The lights dimmed completely, and the curtain opened. He knew he was courting trouble, sitting here in the darkened theater holding Diana's hand. He should go back to his seat before her mother came back. He should let go of her hand and dash out of the box for both of their sakes. But at that moment, nothing would move his hand from hers. Not even an act from God Himself.

"Darling, I do apologize," Elizabeth said when Diana met her in the lobby after the play was over. Her mother looked very contrite. "I know I should have come back to the box straightaway, but you won't believe who I ran into at intermission. Millicent Chenilworth."

Diana had no idea who Millicent Chenilworth was, but she said a silent thank you to the woman for distracting her mother from the play, thus allowing Gavin to remain in her seat for almost the entire second act.

Asking him to stay had been a risk, and he'd delighted her by being willing to take it. He had stayed until the last possible minute, then retreated back to his box seat. During the performance neither of them spoke, both pretending to watch the travesty masquerading as a play unfold on the stage. But they had held hands the entire time, something Diana was acutely aware every single second.

What on earth had possessed her to hold his hand? But she knew the answer. His story had moved her deeply, that was for sure. But it wasn't just out of sympathy or pity that she'd reached out to him. When she told him she had to touch him, her words had been truth. The loneliness she had felt for so long—not only since William had died but also when he was alive—had come flooding over her. She needed the contact, and she needed it from him. When he'd so easily obliged her, a thrill had shot straight from her hand to her toes.

She was falling for him, and she was powerless to overcome it.

Right before he left, he'd planted the barest of kisses on the back of her hand, sending pleasant tingles shooting up her arm. She could still feel them even as she listened to her mother drone on about her friend's latest medical troubles, a topic that seemed to be of infinite interest to anyone over the age of fifty.

"My goodness, I didn't know Gavin Parringer was here."

At the sound of Gavin's name, Diana tuned in to her mother's conversation. She followed Elizabeth's line of sight and saw Gavin and another shorter, older man approaching them. Seamus, she assumed. She also noticed her mother checking the state of her chapeau. Twice.

"Good evening, ladies," Gavin said, giving them a small bow and behaving as if they were meeting for the first time. He winked at Diana right before straightening to his full height.

"Good evening, Lord Tamesly." Elizabeth pulled out her fan, even though it was far from warm in the building. She started to briskly swish it back and forth, waiting for Gavin to make the introductions.

"Lady Elizabeth Dymoke, Mrs. Diana Garland, allow me to introduce you to Dr. Seamus Burns. He is a good friend of mine who has accompanied me from India."

"Pleasure to meet you," Seamus said in his Scots brogue. He nodded politely at Diana, then lifted Elizabeth's hand and placed a kiss on it.

Diana thought her mother was about to faint. Not from taking offense at his bold gesture, but from enjoying the attention. She looked from her mother to Seamus, then back to her mother again. Goodness, the woman was completely smitten.

"A pleasure to meet you, Dr. Burns." Elizabeth's voice sounded slightly breathy.

"Seamus, my lady, if you please."

"Seamus," she said slowly, as if savoring his name.

Diana glanced at Gavin, who also didn't miss the sparks flying between the two. He stepped away from his friend and stood next to Diana. They both observed the other couple as they continued to make each other's acquaintance.

"I would be most delighted if you would allow me to escort you two lovely lasses to your carriage," Seamus said.

"We accept." Elizabeth put her fan over her mouth when she realized how eager she sounded. "I mean . . . that would be quite nice, Seamus."

Allowing Seamus and Elizabeth to lead them out of the theater, Gavin and Diana hung back a few steps. "They seem to be getting along smashingly," Gavin remarked in a lowered voice.

"They are. Although I am surprised your friend would be so forward with a stranger. My mother could be married for all he knows."

"Oh, he knows she is not. He asked me about her the moment we saw you two together."

Diana looked up at Gavin, a slow grin stretching across her face. "Really?"

He nodded. "Seamus is nothing if not ambitious, at least if it is something he wants badly enough."

Pretending to be shocked, she said, "Are you saying that he *wants* my mother?"

"I am saying he wants to get to know her. And from the looks of it, she seems to want the same thing."

As they exited the theater, Diana observed Seamus and her mother speaking animatedly as they stood in front of their carriage. The door was wide open, with their driver standing discreetly to the side. Still, her mother made no move to enter the vehicle.

"We might be here for awhile," Diana commented.

"That would be fine with me." Gavin smiled. "By the way, did I mention to you how much I enjoyed the play? Especially the second act. In fact, I wouldn't mind a repeat performance, if you are so inclined."

Diana returned Gavin's smile with a radiant one of her own. "I would definitely be so inclined." Warning signals went off in her head, but she ignored them. She didn't know what compelled her to be so eager to be in his company, but she didn't regret following her heart.

Obviously he didn't either.

Chapter Ten

"I think there is something wrong with Mother," Emily said.

Diana placed a purple plumed hat on her head and looked in her vanity mirror. She and Emily were getting ready for an afternoon of shopping on High Street. She regarded her reflection. The hat was definitely too much. Taking it off, she then turned and looked at her sister, who was seated on the chair next to the window, waving her fan briskly in front of her flushed face. "Why do you say that?"

"She's been acting strangely lately. Forgetful, like she's preoccupied with something. Do you know she actually forgot that we were supposed to have tea together yesterday? She's never done that before."

Hiding her smile, Diana readjusted one of the pearl-encrusted hairpins that had pulled loose when she took off the hat. She knew the reason behind her mother's change in behavior, but she didn't want to say anything to Emily. Four days had passed since she and her mother had encountered Gavin and Seamus at the theater, and on the carriage ride home her mother had been positively swoony over Seamus. It tickled Diana to see her mother acting so giddy, an emotion Diana had been intimately familiar with the past two days. Her mother wasn't the only one experiencing the effects of a handsome man's attention.

But she kept all of that inside her. To even hint at a possible romantic relationship with Gavin would send Emily into meddling overdrive. Diana imagined the repercussions would be even worse if she knew about her mother's infatuation with Seamus.

"Dear heavens, it is hot in here." Emily rose awkwardly from her chair and threw open the bedroom window, stood in front of it, still waving her fan. "I hope you do not mind, but I am melting from the heat."

"I do not mind a bit." Diana thought the temperature of the room to be quite comfortable, but she didn't want Emily to suffer. "I can use the fresh air."

"Splendid. Now, back to mother . . . my goodness, what a beautiful rose. I've never seen such a shade of lavender before." Emily rose from her chair and walked a few steps to the vase situated on Diana's bedside table. "I cannot believe I did not notice this when I came in." She leaned forward and sniffed a large rose. "It smells heavenly. Where did you get it?"

"It was delivered yesterday afternoon."

"Who gave it to you?"

Diana shrugged, reaching for a simple off-white hat. After placing it on her head, she nodded her satisfaction. A good choice for an afternoon outing.

Emily came over and stood next to her, her irritated expression reflected in the mirror. "I hate when you do that."

"Wear a hat?"

"Not that. I hate when you do not answer my questions."

"But I did." Diana adjusted her hat. Sometimes she couldn't resist frustrating Emily for the fun of it. She winked at her sister in the mirror.

"You are the most exasperating person I know."

"You said that about Michael just last week. I am glad to hear I have dethroned him."

"Ohhhh," Emily blustered. "Why will you not tell me who sent you the flower?"

Diana turned in her chair and looked up at Emily. "Because I have no idea who did."

"Really?" Emily cocked a light-blond brow. "There was no note?"

"No." Although Diana had her suspicions. The mysterious sender had to be Gavin. There was no other possibility, and the romantic gesture was something he would do. However, she wouldn't admit that to Emily. Her feelings for Gavin weren't something she wanted to share with her sister, no matter how much she cared for her.

Emily grinned. "How mysterious. Perhaps you have a secret admirer."

Diana scoffed. "You are letting your imagination get ahead of you, dear sister. It's only one rose, for goodness' sake. Maybe someone made a mistake in the delivery."

"Then why did you not send it back?"

"Because I do not know who to send it to." Such a simple, but elegant gift. Sometimes one perfect rose said so much more than a dozen inferior blossoms. Gavin had such wonderful taste.

"I seriously doubt someone would have purchased one rose and have it sent to the wrong person."

"Mistakes happen." Diana rose from her chair and reached for her reticule.

"And I am sure he would have included a note."

"Um hmmm."

Emily sighed. "You seem awfully disinterested in this. Are you sure you do not know who sent you the rose?"

"We should be on our way, should we not?"

With a suspicious look, Emily stood. "Fine, I will drop the subject. For now. But I think you should consider tracking down who sent the rose. That way if it is a mistake, you could rectify it. And if it is not . . ." She wiggled her eyebrows.

Diana shook her head at her sister's facial antics. "Honestly, you are hopeless."

"Funny, that is what Michael says."

A few moments later, the women were ready to walk out the door and embark on their afternoon shopping trip when the bell sounded. Davies immediately appeared and opened the door.

"How odd," the butler said, stepping out on the front step and looking from left to right, then back again.

"Who is it, Davies?" Diana asked, walking toward the opened door.

"There is no one here, Mrs. Garland. Wait, what is this?" He bent over and picked up a wrapped package, then stepped back inside and closed the door. He held the long, narrow box out to Diana.

Diana accepted the exquisitely wrapped package. She looked for a tag or label that would identify the sender or receiver, but just as with the flowers, there was nothing.

"Did you get another gift?" Emily asked, coming alongside Diana.

"I do not know."

"Do not just stand there, Diana. Open it!" Emily's eyes lit with curiosity. "Oh, this is so exciting!"

"Do not be so overdramatic, Emily. This could be a box of beeswax for all we know."

"Wrapped like that? I hardly think so."

Diana didn't think so either. She had to admit she was just as intrigued and excited as her sister. She fingered the delicate gold ribbon encasing the box.

"What are you waiting for?" Emily said, tapping her foot.

"You really have lost any semblance of patience, haven't you?"

Emily rolled her eyes. "Now you are trying to exasperate me. Fine, if you refuse to open it, then I will."

But when Emily tried to snatch the package away, Diana beat her to it. "All right, I will open it."

"Finally." She looked over Diana's shoulder.

Diana untied the gold ribbon and carefully opened the silver-foil paper to reveal a cream-colored box. She lifted the lid and smiled. Lying in a bed of red satin was a single long-stemmed, pale pink rose.

"Another one?" Emily asked. "Oh, it is so very lovely."

Diana agreed. Gently she lifted the delicate rose and touched one of the petals to her cheek.

"There is something else in the box," Emily pointed out.

Glancing down Diana saw a small, folded piece of paper tucked in between the satin fabric and the side of the box. She replaced the flower and took the paper. Handing the box to Emily, she opened the note.

"You are as beautiful and as perfect as this rose. Please accept this as a small token of my admiration and affection."

"Is it signed?"

"No," Diana said, rereading the note and savoring each word. She couldn't help but smile.

"Still think you do not have an admirer?" Emily said, with a cluck of her tongue.

Her face warming even further, Diana said, "I guess I do."

"I wonder who it is?"

She took the flower from Emily and merely smiled.

"Did you enjoy your outing, my lord?"

Gavin handed his hat and walking cane to the new butler he had recently hired. "I did, Devon. Thank you for asking. Is Seamus here?"

"I am afraid not, sir. He left early this morning, but did not say where he was going or when he would return."

"He has been doing a lot of that as of late." Gavin suspected the reason behind his sudden disappearance during the day had more to do with Diana's mother, Elizabeth, than just reacquainting himself with the sights of London. He smiled. The man deserved some happiness, and from what he could tell, Elizabeth Dymoke was a fine woman. She had borne Diana, after all. "Ah, well, Seamus is a grown man," he said to Devon. "He can come and go as he pleases. He does not to need to check in with me."

"As you say, my lord." Devon hung Gavin's outerwear in the closet near the front door, then picked up a small silver tray from a tall, round table nearby and held it out to Gavin. "You received a letter today."

Gavin lifted the creamy envelope from the tray, inhaling the faint scent of perfume. He recognized it immediately. Diana's. "Thank you, Devon. That will be all."

"Yes, my lord."

Devon left the foyer and Gavin walked to his study, discreetly giving the envelope another sniff. He smiled. It had been a few days since that glorious time he'd held her hand at the theater, and since then she had consumed his thoughts. He was gratified to know she had been thinking about him too.

It had taken every bit of his self-control not to pay her a visit, but he wanted to tread carefully. He didn't want to do anything that might put her off or make her uncomfortable. Although he knew there were rules about how a man approached a woman, he couldn't remember many of them and was afraid of making a misstep.

He'd also some trepidation about pursuing Diana at all, up until the night at the theater. She couldn't have been any bolder in showing her interest. If she were willing to take their newly minted friendship down a different path, than who was he to refuse? He'd told her his story, and that hadn't put her off. If anything, it had drawn them closer together.

Once he'd sat behind his desk, he looked at the letter. His name and title were written in a small, but very feminine script. Sliding his finger underneath the flap of the handmade envelope, he opened it and read the brief note inside.

Mrs. Diana Garland requests the pleasure of your company for tea, tomorrow at five in the evening.

Gavin scribbled his reply, then folded the note and tapped it to his lips. An invitation for tea with Diana. He didn't even bother checking his schedule to see if he was free. He wouldn't miss this opportunity for the world.

Chapter Eleven

For the first time since she could remember, Diana was nervous about receiving a gentleman caller.

Her hand had trembled when she'd written the invitation to Gavin. Even in her carefree youth she had never been this forward with a man before. First she initiated their hand-holding at the theater, and now she was having him over for tea. Without a formal chaperone, although all rules of propriety would be strictly followed. Besides, she was a woman of thirty-three, not a young girl just having her debut. She was certainly entitled to have a friend over for tea.

Although if she were completely honest with herself, something she had not been as of late, she knew Gavin was far from a mere friend.

She went into the kitchen to make one last check of

the meal her cook had prepared. The fragrant aroma of lamb pie tickled her nose as the still-hot filling bubbled beneath the flaky crust. There was also the lighter fare of cheese sandwiches, chocolate biscuits, and fresh strawberries. Everything looked and smelled delectable.

Leaving the kitchen she went to the sitting room, where the tea would be served. Honor, her maid, was fluffing a pillow on the couch. White wax candle tapers burned in a small, elegant candelabra situated on a small table in the middle of the room. The sideboard against the wall across from the fireplace held a pot of steaming tea, and two carafes contained lemonade and milk.

Diana surveyed the room, then realized something was missing. "Honor, would you please go to my room and retrieve the flowers by my bed?"

"Yes, Mrs. Garland."

When her maid had left, Diana put her hand over her stomach, trying to stem the butterflies that were fluttering and flitting inside her. She was positive Gavin was her secret admirer, especially after receiving the second rose. The flowers and the note bespoke of romance, and she knew Gavin was quite the romantic.

Besides, she didn't want it to be anyone else.

"Here they are," Honor said as she entered the room. "Still beautiful. Where would you like me to put them?"

Diana looked around for a few moments before making a decision. "How about there," she said, pointing to an end table near one of the sofas.

When the flowers were in place, Diana heard the front bell. Her heart jumped to her throat, and she touched her cheeks. Drat, they were warm, and she was sure they were redder than she would have liked. Nothing she could do about it now. Smoothing her skirts, she waited for her butler to see her guest in.

But to her horror, it wasn't Gavin who strode into the room. "Colin! What are you doing here?"

Colin jerked his head back a little at her verbal vehemence. "I am visiting my sister, that is what. Why else would I be here?"

"Now?"

"I did not realize I needed a special invitation to see you," he said with an exaggerated sniff, obviously pretending to be offended. Then he glanced around the room. "Although it does appear you have extended an invitation to someone."

Diana hurried toward him before he walked any further into the room. "You are right, I am expecting someone. And while I am happy to see you, this is not exactly a good time. So if you do not mind, I would appreciate it if you will take your leave."

He eyed her suspiciously. "You are acting a bit strange, rushing me out so quickly."

"I am not acting strangely!" she said in a strangled voice.

"You just proved my point. You appear as nervous as a fox being chased by hounds. Who are you entertaining? I have never known you to shoo me out of your home before. Is there something wrong?"

Bother, but her brother was stubborn. And nosy. Though she shouldn't have expected anything less from him. Since their father had died he had taken on the role of his sisters' protector. "Nothing is wrong, Colin, I assure you." She put her hand on his arm. "Now please, if you will excuse me, my company is about to arrive at any moment."

He held up his hand, palm facing toward her. "All right, all right, I will go . . . after you tell me who you are taking tea with."

"For the love of—why do you want to know?"

"Why are being so secretive?"

"I am not being secretive."

"Then tell me who is coming to tea."

The front bell rang again. Diana brought her fingertip to her brow and closed her eyes for a brief moment. Their argument was now a moot point.

Colin grinned in triumph. "Ha. Guess I will find out soon enough."

"Fantastic." So far the evening had gone off to a smashing start.

Davies showed up at the doorway. "Lord Tamesly sent a note saying he will be a little tardy, Mrs. Garland. He sends his regrets, but he will be here as soon as he can."

For the second time in a few minutes, disappointment threaded through her. Bad enough her brother wouldn't leave, but now she had to wait to see Gavin. "Thank you for letting me know, Davies."

"Yes, Mrs. Garland."

After Davies left, Colin's mouth dropped open. "Gavin? That is who you are having for tea? But why would you not tell me . . . wait a minute." He started laughing.

"Stop it," Diana muttered. "I do not see what is so funny."

"Perhaps not funny," Colin said, his laughter fading a bit. "But definitely ironic."

"Listen, you said you wanted us to help Gavin regain his memory. I am doing my part." The excuse was hollow, and Colin clearly saw through it.

"Yes, but I did not expect you to have him over for tea. A very fancy tea, from what I can see. A lot of thought and preparation went into this."

Crossing her arms, Diana said, "So?"

"You never went to all this trouble for him in the past. In fact, you never went to any trouble." His countenance turned serious. "What has changed?"

"Nothing," she said, but averted her gaze.

"You are lying."

She glanced up at him, dropping her arms. "Colin, he will be here any second. This really is not the time or the place to discuss this. I will be more than happy to explain everything to you tomorrow."

"Oh, you will explain, but I doubt you will be happy about it."

Irritation rose inside of her. "Lest you forget, *little* brother, I actually do not owe you any explanations."

"And lest you forget, *big* sister, I still care about you." He reached out and put his hands on her shoulders. "And I care about Gavin."

"You are afraid I will hurt him. Like I did in the past."

"I know you did not hurt him on purpose. But I remember you telling me once that there was nothing between you and Gavin. If I recall correctly, you said there were no sparks." He gave her a half-smile. "At the time I did not understand what you were talking about, but now that I have Lily, I understand completely. And you were right. There needs to be passion, a deep connection between a man and a woman, in order to make things work. You did not have that with Gavin. You did have it with William."

A tightness formed in her chest. Of course Colin would think that of her and William. She hadn't let him know anything different. Her pride had kept her from doing so. How could she admit to anyone, even her family, that her marriage had been a sham? Marrying William had been the biggest mistake of her life, but one she had made herself. No one had forced her to marry him. Thus she had to accept the consequences of that decision, and she had been determined to face them alone.

She turned away. Although she'd never expected to have such a personal conversation with her brother, she found herself wanting to talk to him about Gavin. Maybe if she had been more open about William she might have been spared so much pain. "I cannot explain it, Colin. I know that I did not feel anything for Gavin in the past."

"But just think if you had. Then you would have never met William, and you would have never had such a wonderful marriage."

Tears sprang to her eyes, but they were tears of regret, not grief. If she hadn't been such a fool, she would have listened to Gavin and saved years of heartache. Gavin wouldn't have left, and he wouldn't have lost his memory. Oh, what her vanity and stubbornness had cost her.

"Diana?" Her brother came up behind her and put his hands on her shoulders. "Are you all right?"

She wiped her eyes before turning around, then smiled as brightly as she could. "Yes, Colin. I am fine."

"You are crying. I am so sorry. I did not mean to bring up William to cause you pain. That was thoughtless of me."

"That is all right, Colin. And I am fine, truly."

Relief crept into his eyes. "I am glad. You are a strong woman, Diana. Stronger than most. I think William saw that in you."

She doubted William saw anything but her outward

appearance, just as all men did. Even Gavin. But there was something different about him now. Maybe it was maturity, or maybe it was the hope that he saw beyond her surface to the woman underneath.

"Well, enough about William," Colin said. "What I want to know is this—what is going on between you and my best friend?"

She rubbed her hands together, surprised to find her palms were damp. "I do not know, Colin. But there is something between us. I cannot explain why, or how it came about, just that it is there."

"Do you love him?"

"I have feelings for him, yes. That is all I can tell you, because that is all I know. But if this means anything . . ." She stopped herself, almost admitting she had never felt such a strong attraction for anyone before. But then Colin would question her feelings for William, and she didn't want to get into that. "I like him, Colin," she said, feeling safe enough to admit that much.

"But what if—"

"I cannot think of what ifs. I can only think of right now." The front bell rang. "And now Gavin is here, and I would appreciate it if you left."

Colin nodded. "I will go out the servants' entrance."

Diana let out a deep breath. "Thank you, Colin."

"Just know one thing, Diana. I love you, and I want you to be happy. If Gavin makes you happy, then you have my blessing. Actually, you have my double blessing, as he is one of the most prime fellows I know—with or without his memory."

She grinned. "I think you are jumping ahead of yourself, but I thank you just the same."

"Lord Tamesly has arrived, Mrs. Garland," Davies announced.

Diana turned toward the butler. "Give me a few minutes, then show him in."

Davies spinned smartly on his heel, then left. Colin shortly followed suit, but not before giving Diana a kiss on the cheek. "Good luck," he said in a low voice so as not to be heard, then slipped out of the room before Gavin could detect him.

As he waited for Diana's butler to return, Gavin straightened his cravat, then checked his grip on the bouquet of posies he had brought for Diana. An unexpected—and most unwelcomed—visit from his cousin Percival earlier that afternoon had made him extremely late. Despite not wanting to, he'd been forced to write the man another pledge just so he could be rid of him. After going over his financials before Percival's untimely arrival, Gavin knew he would have to address the problem of his cousin's penchant for requesting handouts sooner than later.

But he didn't want to think about money or Percival. He wanted to focus on Diana. Even though the evening hadn't gotten off to the start he'd wanted it to, he intended to change that.

The butler appeared. "Mrs. Garland will see you now," the stern-faced man said.

Inhaling deeply, he followed the butler to the drawing room and waited while he was announced. When he walked into the room, he had to pull in another burst of air.

Diana had taken his breath away.

Beautiful didn't begin to describe her. She was like a vision, dressed in a soft and flowing light green gown. Her blond hair was swept high on her head and a strand of simple pearls encircled her slender neck. Her cheeks held a rosy glow, matching the color of her plump lips. His mouth itched to kiss them, but he held his ground, even though it was killing him.

If this is how he felt about Diana when he left for India, no wonder he fled the country.

"Hello," she said softly. "I am glad you could come."

"I apologize for being late." He stood still for a moment, still held by her spell.

"Are those for me?"

Blinking, he looked down at the flowers in his hand. "Oh, yes . . . sorry." He handed them to her. "For you."

"Thank you, they are lovely. I will add them to the other ones." She walked over to a small table and tucked the bouquet inside a vase that already held two long-stemmed roses. His simple bouquet looked out of place and cheap next to the exquisite blooms. He wished he'd chosen something more sophisticated.

Diana turned around and faced him. "Please, come and sit down. Honor will serve tea shortly."

"Thank you. Is there a particular place you would like for me to sit?"

"Right here will be fine." There were plush-looking sofas in the center of the room. She gestured to the smaller one. The scent of roses wafted through his nose as he sat down.

He was pleased when she bypassed the other sofa and sat down beside him. The air was filled with her perfume, a heavenly scent he thought he could breathe in forever. "I am glad you invited me tonight," he said.

"I am glad you could come."

"I think you already said that," he replied with a grin.

She smiled back. "I suppose I did. Would you like anything to drink? We have tea already prepared. Lemonade as well. Or if you prefer something stronger—"

"I am fine," he said. And he was. He didn't need anything to drink or to eat. All he needed was her. Sitting there, with only inches separating them, he knew that she was what he always needed. There had been a hole inside him for eight years, and he thought regaining his memory would fill it. But now he knew that wasn't true. The hole wasn't made by his lost memories.

It was made by his lost love.

The realization hit him straight on, threatening to cut him at the knees. But he forced himself to keep a tight rein on his emotions, no matter how difficult he found it to do. Instead he tried to focus on something benign, anything to take his mind off wanting to take her in his arms and kiss her until the end of time. He suddenly caught sight of the roses again.

"Lovely flowers," he said. The compliment sounded banal, but he had to say something to fill the silence growing between them.

Her expression brightened as she smiled. "Thank you. I positively adore them."

"I've never seen a purple rose before."

Her smile dimmed considerably. In fact, now she looked completely bewildered. Certainly not the response he had expected.

"Did I say something wrong?" he asked.

"You do not recognize them?"

Apprehension suddenly filled him. "Should I?"

"Did you not give them to me?"

"If I did, I am sorry, I do not remember it."

She sprang up from the couch, clearly upset now. "I thought you said your amnesia only affected your distant memories."

"It does." He stood up and stepped in front of her, completely confused by the unexpected shift in conversation and mood. "Diana, what are you going on about?"

"The roses. Did you or did you not send the pink one to me yesterday? Along with a special note? A *very* special note?"

He held up his hands in surrender. "Honestly, Diana, I have no idea what you are talking about."

"What about this?" She pointed at the vase.

"I just gave you those a few minutes ago."

"Not those, the other flower." She stormed over to the vase. "This rose—you did not send it to me three days ago?"

Shaking his head, he said, "I am afraid not."

Her face went white. "Oh, no."

He went to her, alarmed. "What is it?"

"If you did not send me them . . . then who did?"

Chapter Twelve

Diana wished the floor would swallow her whole. Embarrassed didn't begin to describe how she felt at that moment. She had assumed Gavin was her secret admirer, and she had been gravely mistaken. Now that she knew the truth, she felt beyond foolish.

"Someone has been sending you roses?" Gavin asked, his confusion apparent on his face.

"Yes. I received the pink one yesterday and the lavender one two days before."

"And you thought they were from me."

"Yes. There was no indication of the sender, you see, and, well we did hold hands at the theater. So I thought . . ." Heat suffused her face.

He nodded slowly, as if trying to absorb the

situation. "So you invited me for tea to thank me for the flowers. That I did not give you."

This couldn't have been more awkward. "Um, yes. That sums everything up very nicely."

He turned around and walked to the vase of flowers. He looked at them for a moment, touching one of the soft rose petals. "They are exquisite," he said after a long moment. "I wish I had sent them." Turning to her, he added, "But I did not."

"I realize that now. I should not have jumped to conclusions."

As walked back toward her, he rubbed the back of his neck. "And I should not have assumed."

"Assumed what?"

"That I would be the only man interested in you. Obviously there is someone else vying for your affections."

His disconcerted expression concerned her. "If there is, I do not know his identity. And I do not care."

He arched a brow. "You are not curious?"

"No."

"Not even a little?"

"Not a smidge." She walked toward him and looked up into his face. His green eyes were filled with wariness, and she sought to relieve him of it. "Gavin, if you did not give me the roses, then I do not want them."

"Diana," he said, his words floating on a whisper. Then he closed his eyes, as if he were fighting a battle inside himself.

"What is wrong, Gavin? You can tell me."

When he opened his eyes, they were bright. "I wish I could remember what I did wrong."

She was confused. "You have done nothing wrong."

"Not now. Eight years ago. I have no idea what I did to drive you from me. Whatever it was, I do not want to do it again. But I am terrified that I will."

Her heart swelled inside her chest as she saw the mixture of fear and longing in his eyes. "It was not you," she whispered. "It was me."

He scoffed. "You do not have to lie for my sake, Diana."

"I promise you, I am not. Gavin, I never gave you a chance. I was a spoiled, selfish girl that thought she had men eating out of her hand. I toyed with your emotions. I led you on." A lump formed in her throat. "I rejected you."

He shook his head. "I cannot believe you would do something like that."

"I did. I can redeem myself a little by saying that I did not let it go on for very long, but I allowed you to think that we had a chance together, when we did not. It shames me to admit it, but that is the truth."

"Then what is different?" he asked. He suddenly stepped away, his expression guarded. "Or are you toying with me again? Telling me about your secret admirer, making sure I know I have competition. Is that your new game?"

"No!" She moved to him, until they were almost

touching. "Please, Gavin. You have to believe me. I would never play you for a fool. I am not the same woman I was eight years ago. I have not been interested in any man since . . . since William died." Pausing, she licked her lips. "Not until now."

He studied her for a moment, and slowly his countenance changed, softened. "I do believe you, Diana. God help me, I do." He cupped her cheek with his hand.

She leaned into his touch and closed her eyes. His hand was warm, strong. She felt him drawing her face toward his, and she readied herself for his kiss. A kiss she knew in her heart would change her for the rest of her life.

"Mrs. Garland?"

They jumped apart at the sound of Honor's tentative voice.

"Tea is ready."

Gavin silently blasted the maid's timing. He had been seconds away from kissing Diana, a kiss he would have surely enjoyed beyond words. Putting his hands behind his back, he clenched them into fists, feeling cheated.

Diana cleared her throat and smoothed back her perfectly coiffed hair, as if they had been caught in something more illicit than an almost-kiss. She directed the maid to put the tray laden with food on the sideboard.

Once the young woman had completed her task,

she turned and looked at her mistress, her expression as blank as a white page. "Will that be all?"

"Yes, Honor, thank you."

"My pleasure." She turned and started to leave the room.

"Oh, and Honor?"

The young woman spun around and looked at Diana.

"Make sure you keep the door open."

"Yes, Mrs. Garland."

After the maid left, Diana collapsed onto the sofa into a fit of giggles. Gavin joined her, although he didn't see what was so amusing.

"Would you like to clue me in on the joke?"

She wiped her eyes and looked at him. "I know, I should not be laughing. I should be terrified that Honor will blab to everyone that she caught you taking advantage of me at tea time."

"I was hardly taking advantage of you."

"But you were thinking about it, were you not?"

He opened his mouth to speak, then grinned. "I cannot tell a lie. I was thinking about it. But that is a far cry from actually doing such a thing. And I assure you, Diana, I respect you—"

"Far too much to take advantage of me." She chuckled, then smiled widely.

"Ah. You have heard that before."

"Yes, many times. But I hardly ever believed the gentlemen when they said it."

"And now?" he said, leaning forward. "Do you believe me?"

"I more than believe you, Gavin. I trust you." And in that moment, she realized she did. After years of being unable to trust anyone other than her family, she knew she could put her faith in Gavin. "In my estimation," she said, trying to keep her voice from trembling, "that is far more important."

He let out an exaggerated sigh, then stood up. "I suppose since there will be no taking advantage of anyone tonight, we should have a bite to eat." He held out his hand. "Is that lamb I smell?"

She slipped her hand in his. "Yes, it is. The best lamb pie you will ever partake of."

"Oh, I am not so sure about that." He tucked her hand in the crook of his arm and led her to the sideboard. "You forget I lived in India. I have partaken of some very tasty lamb dishes."

"Then you will have to judge for yourself. Allow me." She picked up a plate, then cut into the lamb pie, serving him a healthy portion. Just as he accepted it, they were interrupted again, this time by Davies.

"Mrs. Garland, I am terribly sorry for the intrusion, but you have received another package."

Diana turned and looked at him. "Thank you for telling me, Davies. I will take a look at it in the morning."

"Wait a minute." Gavin set down his plate and walked to the butler. "Did you see who delivered it?"

"No, my lord. There was a knock on the door, so faint that if I had not been walking past the door at that precise moment I would not have heard it. When I opened the door, the package was on the doorstep, but there was no one in sight."

"Just like yesterday," Diana said.

"Bring the package here," Gavin commanded.

Diana shook her head. "I already told you, Gavin. I do not want it."

"You do not have to keep it, Diana. But maybe there is another clue as to the identity of the sender."

"Does it really matter?"

Gavin looked at her. "Yes, it does to me. I want to find out who this chap is. That way I can tell him to stop sending you gifts. And believe me, I will tell him in quite a forceful way."

Her lips quirked a smile as she took the package from Davies. Quickly she ripped off the paper and opened the box, which resembled the same case as the one that had arrived yesterday. Nestled inside was another rose—a vibrant orange one. Beside it lay a small note. When she didn't pick it up, he did.

"My passion for you burns like a fiery flame," he read aloud. "Please accept this as a symbol of my passion for you." He looked at Diana. "Whoever this chap is, he is no poet."

"I do not care who he is," she said, then frowned. An unexpected shiver passed through her.

He went to her. "Are you all right?"

She looked up at him with wary eyes. "It was one thing to receive these roses and notes, thinking they were from you. But now that I know they are not, I find it quite disturbing." Placing the lid back on the box, she tossed it on the floor. "I will have Davies dispense with it in the morning."

"I think that is a good idea." He hesitated for a brief second, then spoke again. "I know you said you did not want to know who sent these, but *I* do. Especially since this is upsetting you. Would you mind if I took the note and made some inquiries?"

Shaking her head, she said, "No. By all means. Although I do not know how that note can be of any help."

He put the slip of paper in his pocket, wondering the same thing. Still, he couldn't let someone send Diana roses and not at least try to discover the man's identity. "You will let me know if you receive anything else, right?"

"Absolutely." She looked down at her hands and wrung them together. "But what if . . . what if he's not satisfied with just sending roses?"

Moving close to her, he put his finger on her chin and lifted it up. "I promise you, Diana, whoever this man is, I will not let him hurt you. I swear my life on it."

Relief flowed over her features. "I believe you, Gavin." She took his hand and pressed her cheek against it.

The feel of her skin against his palm was nearly his undoing. With great effort he pulled his hand away from her cheek. "I do not think you should mention to anyone that you received another gift. Not until we get to the bottom of this."

"My lips are sealed."

At the mention of her lips, his gaze immediately went to her mouth. "You should not have said that," he murmured, partly in jest, partly serious.

Her cheeks took on a rosy hue, making her all the more beautiful. "We should finish our meal, do you not think?"

Even though eating was the last thing from his mind, he was far too much of a gentleman to entertain the devilish thoughts at the fringe of his brain. Shoving them away, he nodded reluctantly and said, "Lead me to the lamb, if you please."

Chapter Thirteen

The morning after taking tea with Diana, Gavin rose bright and early. After a light breakfast he entered his study and went straight for his desk. Opening the top drawer, he took out the note from Diana's mystery admirer. He had placed it in the drawer the night before, after he had returned from her home. Settling into the chair, he examined the paper, not knowing what he was looking for. A detective he was not, nor did he know anyone. Perhaps Buttons might be able to refer someone. Until then, he stared at the uneven script, as if willing the handwriting to reveal its composer.

Silence.

With a frustrated sigh he set the paper aside. The fact that she had another man interested in her, apparently deeply interested in her, greatly unnerved him.

He hadn't even officially declared his intentions to her, although they were plainly obvious. The last thing he wanted or needed was competition. Despite her reassurances that she wasn't swayed by the extravagant gifts, he didn't want to give this man any opportunity to woo her further.

Putting the mystery man out of his mind for the moment, he tuned in to the ledger on his desk and started calculating. He was deep into the numbers when his butler appeared.

"Percival Parringer is here to see you, my lord."

Gavin's shoulders slumped from the strain of bending over the desk, and from hearing about his cousin's arrival. This was the third week in a row the man had dropped by without an invitation, and Gavin knew exactly what he was after. Rubbing his tired eyes, he motioned for Devon to let Percival in.

Moments later his cousin entered the room. "Good morning, Gavin," he said, his tone bright. When he smiled he revealed a set of teeth yellowed from smoke and drink. "How are you this fine morning?"

"Weary," Gavin replied, hoping Percival would get to the point of his visit and dispense with the false pleasantries. "What can I help you with?"

"You are assuming I need something?"

"Do you not always?"

Percival's smile faltered. "Yes, well, you are right. I was hoping you could see your way to extending your loan."

"The time or the amount?"

"Both, actually."

"Creditors still hounding you?"

"Oh, yes, they are relentless." Percival wrung his hand together.

Gavin couldn't help but perceive the gesture as greedy. This was the second time his cousin had asked for more money, and he wondered if it would ever end. From what he had been able to gather, Percival lived a precarious existence, one filled with gambling and other vices. The man had no concept of earning money, only of spending it.

The time had come to put an end to the handouts. Gavin looked up at his cousin, noticing the yellowish stain on his cravat where it touched the skin of his neck. The man not only had ill habits, he had poor hygiene as well. "I am afraid I cannot agree to your request, dear cousin."

Percival's mouth dropped open. "Why the devil not?"

Rising from his chair, Gavin leaned over the desk. "Please understand, this is for your own good. You need to stand on your own feet, Percival. Find a way to pay your creditors back on your own."

"I—I cannot do that!"

"Why not?"

Clouds formed behind Percival's sallow eyes. "It is so easy for you, is it not? Sitting behind that desk, acting as if you care about me."

"I do," he said. "I care about your welfare. You are family."

"Then treat me like family!"

"I am treating you like a human being. Percival, you are a wreck. You look like you have not slept in days, you reek of drink, and your clothes are in shambles."

Percival's eyes flashed. "That is because I have no money!"

"No, it is because you spend whatever money you have." Gavin looked down and searched the surface of his desk. Locating the paper he sought, he held it up. "Perhaps we can compromise. Here are the Tamesly holdings in Lancashire. I will deed this over to you—"

Percival's features relaxed. "Thank you—"

"—with the caveat that you move to Lancashire to oversee the property and the tenants. Whatever proceeds you earn are yours to do with as you please."

"That is blackmail."

"No, cousin. That is *business.*"

Clenching his fists, Percival pounded one of them on the desk. "You cannot deny me my due!"

Gavin stepped back, stunned. The man standing before him was of a completely different character than the one that had first approached him, practically begging him for money. "I am not denying you your due. I am giving you land, for bloody sakes."

"And requiring me to leave London."

"Yes, that is true. How else are you to ably manage the estate?"

"Many lands have been managed from London. There needs not be a lord present."

"In this case, there does," Gavin countered. "The estate has been dreadfully mishandled in my absence."

"How do you know that occurred during your absence?" Percival sneered. "Perhaps it was in a shambles because of your own doing!"

Gavin paused, knowing his cousin could be right. "Is that true?"

Percival hesitated the slightest bit. "Yes."

Gavin didn't believe him, but decided to go along with the ruse. "Then this is your opportunity to fix my mistakes."

Squaring his shoulders, Percival stated, "I am not leaving London."

"Then you will not get a single pence from me until you show me you can be fiscally responsible."

Fury emanated from the man. "You will pay for this," he gritted out. "I will see to it."

Sitting back down, Gavin said calmly, "You do that." He didn't acknowledge Percival further, didn't even look up until he heard his footsteps retreating, then finally disappearing out of the room.

Slumping over his desk, Gavin dropped his head into his hands. Outwardly he had appeared cool and unruffled to his cousin, but inwardly he shook to his core. He had been right to stand up to Percival, and his offer had not been unreasonable. He had no regrets about that. But the angry and threatening response he had received from his cousin caused his guard to fire up. He had little doubt Percival would at least try to follow through with his threat.

He also knew he had to watch his own back.

"I believe it is time you threw a party."

Gavin had been in the middle of putting a forkful of Yorkshire pudding in his mouth when Seamus made his suggestion. He paused, his fork hanging in midair. "I should do what?"

"A party. Just a small gathering. We could even make it a celebration of your return to London."

Thinking his friend had lost complete control of his senses, Gavin set down his utensil. "Seamus, have you noticed the state of this house? It is not exactly party-ready."

"Poppycock," Seamus said, leaning back in his chair. He crossed his hands over his full belly. " 'Twould only take a few days of spit and polish to make this place shine."

"Why are you such a festive mood all of the sudden?"

"Do I need a reason, lad?" He sat forward and smiled.

Gavin didn't miss the twinkle in his eye. "Me thinks I know the answer," he said, imitating his friend's burr.

"You do?"

"Aye. This has to do with a fair lassie, does it not?"

"Your accent needs help," Seamus said good-naturedly.

"Ah, the man does not deny it."

"Nay, I do not. I am too old for games, lad, and I fully admit that I have my eye on the sweet Elizabeth Dymoke. Just as you have your eye on her fair daughter."

Gavin opened his mouth to protest, but then snapped it shut. There was no reason to deny his feelings for Diana, especially not from Seamus, who wouldn't believe him anyway. "Perhaps a party would be a good idea," he said, mulling the prospect over. It would help him keep his mind off of Percival. Better yet, he would get to see Diana again. They would talk. And dance. He might even sneak in that kiss he was so cruelly denied a few days ago.

"I will help you with gettin' this place into shape, and, of course, with the guest list."

"Elizabeth will be the first," Gavin assured.

"Nay. Diana will be."

Gavin laughed. "We should invite them at the same time." He rather enjoyed joking around with Seamus about their romantic interests. Here they were, two bachelors, both well past the marrying age, Seamus even more so. There was no reason not to pursue the objects of their affections.

"We will do it," he decided, picking up his fork

again. He took the bit of Yorkshire pudding and thoughtfully chewed. "However, it must be a small affair. Family and close friends." He didn't think he could handle the huge crowd that had been at the Balcarris fete.

"Of course."

"Actually, let's just make it close friends. Forget the family," he added, thinking of Percival again. He hadn't heard from his cousin in several days, and that was fine by him. Hopefully the man had figured out another way to deal with his debts and habits.

The decision made, Gavin and Seamus discussed the party details, but soon found themselves at a loss. Neither of them had thrown a party before. At least Gavin couldn't remember hosting one.

"We need a woman's touch," Seamus said. "Someone to take care of all those bothersome details."

"Are you thinking about Elizabeth?"

Seamus shook his head. "I do not want her planning this, I want her to enjoy it. Same with Diana."

Gavin snapped his fingers. "Mrs. Bloomfield can do it."

"Nay, the poor lassie has enough to do, taking care of the house."

"I have hired extra help, remember?" Gavin said, amused that Seamus called Mrs. Bloomfield a lassie, even though the woman was quite a few years older than he was. The good doctor had a big soft spot for the ladies, no matter their station in life. "Her duties have diminished considerably. I will speak to her about it. I am sure she will not mind."

Once Seamus had agreed with Gavin's idea, the men finished the meal in companionable silence, each one lost in his thoughts. Gavin found himself growing more excited about the prospect of hosting his friends in his home, and especially about seeing Diana. He had thought about her day and night since he last saw her at her house for tea.

He couldn't wait to see her again.

Chapter Fourteen

"You look lovely, Mama."

"You are just being kind, Diana." Elizabeth looked at her reflection in her vanity mirror and frowned. "My face is full of wrinkles."

"It is not." Diana came up behind her mother and knelt down next to her, placing her face against hers.

But instead of smiling, Elizabeth's frown deepened. "Now I definitely look like an old hag."

"Mother!" Diana straightened. "You are *not* an old hag. I do not want to hear you refer to yourself that way again."

Elizabeth sighed. "Oh, all right." She pinched her cheeks until they reddened, then took one last regretful look in the mirror.

Diana had never known her mother to be so on

edge before going to a party before. Granted, this was a special party, thrown by Gavin and Seamus. If her mother hadn't shown how enamored of Seamus she was already, her behavior tonight would have clued even the most obtuse person into her inner feelings.

"Mama, if we do not leave soon we will be late." Diana had been ready for the past half hour, filled with anticipation of seeing Gavin again. She had missed him these past few days, and had hoped he would have paid her a call. Inviting her to a party was even better, and she marveled that she could even admit that to herself, considering just a few weeks ago she had abhorred such social events.

How things had changed in such a short time.

"I think I am ready," Elizabeth said, rising from her chair. She turned to her daughter. "Are you sure I look presentable?"

Diana kissed her mother's still-smooth cheek. "More than presentable. You will sweep Dr. Seamus Burns completely off his feet." Before her mother could protest, Diana sailed out of the room and down the stairs to retrieve her wrap from Blevins.

A short time later they arrived at Gavin's modest, yet tastefully decorated, flat. Diana's stomach flipped and flopped as she entered the foyer, where she was met by Devon, Gavin's butler. The man greeted her and her mother and took their wraps from them. "Lord

Tamesly and Dr. Burns are in the sitting room," he said. "They are awaiting your arrival."

"Thank you," Elizabeth said, then they followed the butler, who announced them before they walked into the room.

They weren't the first to arrive. Colin and Lily were already there, visiting with Michael and Emily. There were a couple other people Diana didn't recognize, and she was glad to see that Gavin had been busy renewing his old acquaintances. He was speaking with a shorter, older man when Devon had introduced them to the group.

Gavin's head turned, and he met Diana's gaze. The smile he gave her warmed her completely to her toes, and made her feel lighter than air. The attraction she felt for this man grew deeper and more intense as time passed. More than anything she wanted to run into his arms and melt in his embrace. Instead, she tamped down her emotions and made her way into the room, trying to appear nonchalant.

Her mother, on the other hand, wasn't as deft at hiding her feelings. As soon as she saw Seamus, she headed straight for him, then giggled when he kissed her hand. Diana couldn't believe her mother had been worried about looking old. At the moment she appeared as young and giddy as a school girl.

Grasping her hand, Seamus suddenly led her to the front of the room. He cleared his throat once, then twice. Finally he said, "May I have your attention."

Diana glanced at Gavin. Even he seemed surprised by Seamus's actions. Elizabeth certainly was. But if Seamus noticed their reaction, he didn't let on.

"Now that you are all here, I have an announcement to make." He took Elizabeth's other hand, held them both in his own, and faced her. "I know I have not known you for long, lass, but I do know my heart. I am an old man—"

"Nonsense," Elizabeth interjected.

"Please, do not interrupt, darlin'. I am nervous enough already." His comment elicited a laugh from the observers. "What I am tryin' to say is that I have never met a woman as beautiful, kind, and lovin' as you, Elizabeth Dymoke. And I would be the happiest man ever if you would do me the honor of becomin' my wife."

A collective gasp sounded throughout the room. Diana looked at Gavin, who appeared shocked. Then she looked at her mother, who also seemed stunned. Tears suddenly streamed down her cheeks. "Oh, Seamus," she said with a sniff. "I would be honored to be your wife!"

"Just a bloody moment," Colin said, striding forward, breaking up the romantic moment. "Do you not think this is a bit sudden?"

"Colin," Lily said, rising to meet her husband.

He ignored her. "Mother, how can you agree to marry this man? You barely know him."

Elizabeth faced her son. "Darling, I appreciate your concern. But I do believe I am of an age to make my own decisions." She turned and gazed at Seamus. "I have been in love with him since the first time we met."

"And I her," Seamus said. He leaned forward and touched his forehead to hers.

"Well, I think this is positively wonderful!" exclaimed Emily, who with some assistance from Michael got up from her chair. She waddled over to her mother and hugged her tightly, then extended her embrace to Seamus. "Welcome to the family," she exclaimed.

Diana observed the tender scene with a smile. She was happy that her mother had found happiness after so many years of widowhood. She looked up and saw that Gavin was staring at her, his eyes filled with warmth.

A short while later, after congratulating her mother and Seamus and spending time visiting with Colin, Lily, Michael, and Emily, Diana escaped outside for some fresh air. Several torches had been lit on the perimeter of the modest patio, casting the area in soft light. The full moon high in the sky added its silvery glow to the magical night. A night filled with declarations of love and promises of the future.

She smiled as she heard footsteps behind her, knowing who they belonged to. Deep down she had hoped Gavin would join her out here. They hadn't had a moment to themselves since the party began. Turning, she saw him standing in the doorway, looking as devastatingly handsome as ever. The cut of his evening suit drew attention to his slim, but muscular physique. His skin had lightened a bit since his return to London, but it still retained a healthy glow. As he approached her, he made sure the door to the patio was kept wide open. Always the gentleman.

"Hello," she said, a sudden and inexplicable shyness coming over her.

"Hello," he said softly in return. Then he came to her and stood beside her. "Interesting evening, wouldn't you say?"

"I definitely would. Did you know about Seamus's plan?"

"No, but I should have suspected something was up. It was his idea to throw the party, a move that is not exactly characteristic of him." He looked at her. "What do you think about what happened?"

"I am very happy for both of them. My mother adores Seamus, and he seems to feel the same way. I am glad she was able to love again after all these years."

He cleared his throat at her words. After a long pause he asked, "And what about you, Diana?"

She gazed up at him. "What about me?"

"I know how much your husband meant to you. Will you . . . will you ever be able to love again?"

Facing him fully, she said without hesitation, "I already have."

His smile made her heart skip several beats. Though

she yearned to be held in his arms, he maintained his distance. Then his smile faded a bit. "But we have not known each other that long."

"Speak for yourself," she teased. "I have known you for over a decade."

But his expression remained serious. "You know what I mean. What I want to know is . . . are you sure?"

"About my feelings for you? Gavin, I have never been more sure of anything in my entire life."

He closed his eyes for a moment. When he opened them, they had darkened to a smoldering green. "I want to kiss you so much right now," he said in a husky voice.

A pleasant shiver coursed through her at his words. "And I very much want you to kiss me."

"But I do not dare," he said, glancing through the open doorway into the house. "If we are caught . . ."

"Would that be such a bad thing?"

"To your brother, yes. And probably to Michael as well. I do not think I could fight them both."

"I doubt that you would have to, but I see your point." She tried to hide her disappointment, but it was difficult.

He turned away and put his hands in his pockets, as if having to force himself not to touch her. "We should go inside. It is dangerous out here."

"I feel quite safe, thank you very much."

"You should not." He turned and looked at her, his eyes filled with desire. "You really should not."

She could barely breathe at the wanting she saw reflected on his face.

"Tell me one thing, Diana Garland."

"Yes?" She sounded breathless.

"If I surprised you with a proposal the way Seamus did with your mother tonight . . . what would be your answer?"

"You already know what my answer would be."

He smiled and said, "Yes. I do."

The next morning Diana woke up, groggy with sleep but happy from having dreamt of Gavin once again. Her body warmed at the memory of their conversation on the patio. They didn't get another chance to speak alone for the rest of the night, but she carried his question in her heart.

What would be your answer?

Without a doubt she would marry him if he asked. She didn't understand or even care how she'd fallen in love with him, she just knew she had. She also knew that he loved her too, even though he hadn't said the words out loud. He had expressed them with the passion in his eyes, the tenderness of his voice. She wasn't some ingénue with no experience fanning the flames of infatuation. She had married before, and it had been a mistake.

Now, with Gavin, she had a second chance.

Just before she had left to go home the night before, Gavin had whispered that he would see her soon. They needed to talk. She knew what he wanted to talk about, and she couldn't wait until she saw him again.

Filled with the warmth of blossoming love, she leaped out of bed, quickly went through her morning routine, and headed down the stairs for breakfast. When she entered the dining room, she surveyed the empty table. For so long she had denied her loneliness, convincing her family and herself that she was fine living alone. Now she understood she had been deceiving herself—out of fear, out of refusing to open her heart to someone else. She hadn't been ready to love, or ready to let go of the hold William's memory had over her. It had tainted everything in her life. Now she wanted to be rid of it.

Knowing what she had to do, she ran to the small study that had been William's office. She rarely entered the room, for the memories were too painful. Taking a deep breath, she opened the door and walked in, breathing in the musty smell that permeated the air from lack of use. Shutting the door behind her, she made her way in the darkness and found the oil lamp and the matches lying next to it. Striking one of them, she lit the lamp, flooding the room with light.

Everything was just as William had left it. His books, neatly arranged by size and catalogued by author and subject, lined one bookcase from floor to ceiling. On the wall behind his desk was a painting of the Lake District. He had loved the water, and often he had taken trips there. To sail, he had said. Little did she know at the time he had been doing much more than sailing on those beautiful waters.

Tears spilled down her cheeks as she thought of him, of how he had betrayed her. The pain that surrounded her heart deepened with so much intensity she didn't think she could stand it. But she had to experience the hurt full force, in order to let it go. To let him go.

It was time she moved on and found happiness. True happiness with a man who only had her best interests at heart, who wouldn't cheat on her and treat her as if she were worthless. Gavin had proven that he was that man in the past, and he had shown her he would be that man in the future.

She had never spoken the words out loud, had never been able to. But now she was ready. She was ready to let him go.

"Goodbye, William," she whispered into the silence. "You cannot hurt me anymore."

Chapter Fifteen

Gavin whistled as he strode down the street toward Diana's house. The sun shone brightly in the cloudless sky, and the temperature was warm, but not uncomfortably so. A perfect day for a walk. The perfect day to see the woman he loved.

They had been apart for eight hours, and he couldn't stand not seeing her any longer. He supposed he should go the formal route and send his card requesting a visit, then wait for her to respond. But that would take far too long, and he had neither the patience nor the desire to spend another minute without her.

He took out his pocket watch and checked the time: three-forty-five. Too late for lunch, but a little early for tea. No matter. He didn't need the excuse of a meal to see her, and he doubted she would refuse him if he showed up unannounced. Such confidence was a foreign concept to him, but he enjoyed it immensely. There was something delightful in knowing that your feelings were being returned.

Although his memories had yet to resurface, he could now imagine the heartache he must have gone through knowing Diana didn't love him. Over the past few hours he'd thought about the bits and pieces he'd learned about his past, and wondered what would have happened if he hadn't left London. Would he have been able to make her fall in love with him? Would he had even tried, knowing she was in love with someone else?

Finally, he realized he was overthinking everything. The past didn't matter anymore. What mattered was the present, and, of course, the future. With Diana by his side, he could face the future with an assurance he would have never thought possible since he had lost his memory. He planned to broach the subject with her as soon as possible.

His heart tripped out of rhythm as he neared her house. Hastening his steps, he headed toward the modest brick home, eager to see her, to talk to her, simply to be with her.

Suddenly he saw a young boy standing on the front step.

"What ho!" Gavin yelled, running toward the child.

The youth dashed off the front step and ran in the opposite direction.

Gavin sprinted after him, catching the boy as soon as he rounded the corner. Grasping his threadbare, rough-textured shirt, Gavin demanded, "What were you doing at Mrs. Garland's home?"

"N-nothing sar," the boy said, stark fear emanating from his eyes.

"Do not lie to me. I saw you on her front step. Now, I will ask you again—what were you doing there?"

"Makin' a delivery, sar."

"Who for?"

"Don't know 'is name. 'E gave me a pence and the box and said put it in front o' the door. Did what 'e tole me an' that's all. I swear!"

Gavin scrutinized the boy, searching his face for a glimpse of deceit. He found none. Releasing the youth he said, "Have you done this for him before?"

He shook his towhead. "No, sar. Never seen 'im afore today."

Stepping back, Gavin dug into his pocket and found a guinea. He flipped it to the boy, who caught it between his grimy hands. "You stay away from that house, understand?"

The youth stared at the coin in his hands. "Yes sar," he whispered, then shot his gaze at Gavin. "Thank ye, sar. Thank ye." He turned and fled down the street, his bare feet slapping against the pebbled road.

Quickly Gavin backtracked to Diana's and saw a familiar box on the step. He picked it up and thought about ringing the bell, but changed his mind. No need to upset her with the unwanted gift. Instead, he decided to take it back to his house and examine the package himself. Turning away, he headed back to his flat.

When he reached his house, he was surprised to see Colin's coach pull up. His friend exited and met him in front of the walk.

"Oh, I am sorry," Colin said. "I see you are leaving."

"Just coming back, actually."

"Ah. Well then, I thought maybe you would like to take in a drink at White's, if you were available this afternoon."

Gavin gave him a half-smile. "Wanting to find out more about Seamus, is that it?"

Colin grinned. "I have never been able to fool you, Gav. Yes, that is my ulterior motive. You would want the same thing, were you in my shoes."

"Of course I would."

Pointing to the box Gavin held, Colin asked, "What is that?"

"This?" Gavin hesitated, not know if he should confide in Colin about Diana's admirer. As her brother he would want to know. But Gavin suspected Diana wouldn't appreciate Colin's interference. "Nothing," he said, deciding to keep his friend in the dark. "Let me drop it off inside and we can go." He would examine the contents when he returned.

"Very well."

The men walked inside the house. Gavin headed

straight for the study, Colin following closely behind. "I will just be a moment—bloody hell!"

Colin came up beside him. "What—good Lord!"

Propped up in front of his desk was his missing portrait—his face slashed to bits.

Diana bent over her latest crewel project and removed the last ten stitches she'd sewn into the fabric. She had stitched this piece three times in the past half hour, but she made mistakes every time. Her concentration on the project wasn't there. How could it be, when all she could think about was Gavin?

She thought she would have heard from him by now. When he'd said he wanted to talk, she assumed it would be soon. Perhaps her idea of soon and his were completely different. Or perhaps she had read more into their conversation than had been there.

Surely she hadn't dreamt that he had brought up marriage. She had gone through their exchange several times over the day, and each time her heart soared. But now her elation had dimmed to a dull ache of impatience. She had half a mind to go visit him herself, but that certainly wouldn't do. They had been fairly forward in their relationship thus far, but there were certain lines she refused to cross.

Folding her crewelwork, she tossed it in the wicker basket next to her chair and stood. Rubbing her neck, she tried to ease the tension that had gathered there, partly from leaning over her needlecraft and partly from disappointment that Gavin hadn't appeared yet. A quick glance outside told her that evening had descended. If he hadn't come by now, he probably wasn't coming at all.

She climbed the stairs to her bedroom, deciding to skip supper. She wasn't hungry anyway. Once she entered her room she sat down at her vanity and pulled the hairpins out of her coiffure, then massaged her scalp as her hair fell down the length of her back. Picking up a hairbrush, she had just run it partway through her hair when a soft knock sounded on her door.

"Yes?" she said, pulling the brush through the rest of her hair.

"Mrs. Garland? A Mr. Parringer is here to see you."

"You mean Lord Tamesly?"

"I think," Honor said through the oak wood door. "Although he said Mr. Parringer."

Diana frowned. Perhaps her maid was confused. She often got titled peers mixed up in the past, and Diana couldn't blame her. Often she couldn't keep all the dukes and earls and whatnot straight either. A frisson of heat passed through her, searing her inside. He had come after all. "Tell him I will be down in a moment, Honor."

"Yes, ma'am."

Feeling sheepish for doubting Gavin, she reached for a hairpin, then changed her mind. It would take far too long to put her hair up again, and she didn't want to call back Honor and ask for her help. Instead, she fastened her hair into a simple braid fastened at the nape of her neck, spritzed on a bit of perfume, pinched her cheeks, and flew downstairs, eager to see Gavin, eager to hear what he had to say.

Not waiting for Davies to announce her, she threw open the door to her sitting room. "I thought you would never come," she said, floating into the room. Then she froze, her mouth dropping open in shock. "What are you doing here?"

Percival Parringer gave her a yellowed grin. "I came to see if you liked my gifts."

Chapter Sixteen

"**I** do not see why you sent for Michael," Gavin said, staring at what was left of his portrait. He could still tell it was his image, but barely. The ragged rips and tears in the canvas bespoke of ferocity. Whoever had wielded the knife had been enraged, that much was clear. "He has nothing to do with this."

"I know," Colin said, standing beside his friend. "But he can help us discover who did this."

"What do you mean?"

"Michael has special connections, so to speak."

"What kind of connections?"

Colin pressed his lips together briefly, then stepped forward, speaking in a conspiratorial manner. "What I am about to tell you must go to your grave. Understand? If it does not, not only is Michael's life in danger, but mine and the rest of my family's as well."

A spasm of anxiety assaulted him at the seriousness of his friend's words. "I will not speak of it," he assured Colin. "You have my word."

"Which is good enough for me. You may have a hard time believing this, but Michael is a spy."

Gavin scoffed. "Michael Balcarris?" He thought about the proper and rather effete looking man who was Colin's brother-in-law. "Are we speaking of the same bloke?"

Colin nodded, his eyes devoid of amusement. "I am."

"I cannot believe this." He sat down in a chair. "Did I know this before?"

"No. Michael kept it a secret from everyone for years. I only found out shortly after I met Lily. Since then I have been his partner of sorts, up until his retirement after he married Emily."

"Does she know?"

"I suspect she does, although we have never spoke of it."

"Who else knows?"

"Lily . . . and now you. That is all, other than the other operatives. Michael is well connected not only here in England, but also throughout the continent. If anyone can ferret out who broke in and destroyed your portrait, he can."

"There really is no need for him to be involved. I already know the culprit." Gavin looked at Colin morosely. "My cousin."

"But why?"

"The man hates me." He gestured to the destroyed portrait. "I think that is obvious."

"I think you are right, if indeed he did this."

"Oh, he did. He had the portrait in his possession. At least that is what he said. Told me he was having it repaired."

"He did a frightfully bad job of it."

Gavin rose from his chair, picked up the portrait, and set it against the wall near his desk. "I am afraid Michael will have wasted a trip over here," he said to Colin.

"You do not sound very upset about this."

"Should I be?"

"Gav, anyone who does something like that is not all there. If I may say so, it seems to me he is trying to send you a message."

"Oh yes, you are right about that."

"And you are not worried?"

Gavin turned around. "Colin, my cousin is harmless. If he thinks he is scaring me by ripping up a portrait I do not even remember sitting for, then he is mistaken. I will just have a new one made."

With a frown Colin said, "I think you are taking this too lightly."

"And you are taking it far too seriously. As it is, Michael is going to be quite peeved at being summoned for nothing. It is not as if he is my biggest fan."

"That is all water under the bridge," Colin said. "Besides, Michael has never met a mystery he did not like . . . or that he could not solve."

"But there is no mystery. Just my incredibly annoying cousin's pathetic attempt to put me off guard."

"Pity," Michael said, striding through the door. "I had so hoped it was something more. I am always in the mood for a mystery."

Gavin spun around to see Michael walk into the room. He almost didn't recognize the man. Despite being overly dressed as usual, there was a difference in his demeanor, posture, and expression. He exuded confidence and authority, and commanded respect. Gavin had no trouble accepting that the man standing in the doorway of his study was a spy, and a well regarded one at that.

Remarkable.

"Well, if there is no mystery, then perhaps I could have a drink instead?" But when he walked into the room, the toe of his shoe clipped a long box on the floor.

Gavin inwardly cursed himself for being so careless as to drop the box, forgetting about it in the shock of seeing his picture shredded.

Michael picked it up, the lid askew. "What is this?"

"Nothing," Gavin said quickly. He crossed the room and took the box from Michael. When he did, the top came completely off.

"A rose?" Michael arched a brow and looked at Colin. "Maybe we have a mystery after all."

"There is nothing mysterious about a flower," Gavin snapped.

"No, but your reaction to said flower is most puzzling."

Gavin shrank back at the inquiring looks Colin and Michael were giving him, feeling like a cornered doe.

"I think I can solve this mystery," Colin said, giving Gavin a knowing look. "That rose is for Diana."

"Yes, you are right." He put the lid back on the box.

"But if that is the case, why are you acting as if it is a secret? I know how you feel about my sister, Gavin, and I give you both my whole-hearted support."

"I appreciate that," Gavin said, silently questioning how Colin had come to that knowledge and vowing to ask him at a later time. He clumsily tried to put the lid back on the box. When he did, he dislodged a small piece of paper loose from inside. It floated to the ground. Before he could catch it, Colin snatched it up off the floor.

"Roses are red," Colin read with an exaggerated flourish.

"Give me that," Gavin demanded.

Colin held it out of his friend's reach and kept reading. "Violets are blue. If I had one wish it would be to . . ." His good humor faded in an instant, replaced with umbrage. He glared at Gavin. "I should shoot you where you stand."

"What?" Gavin asked, bewildered not only at his friend's change in mood but by his remarks.

"How dare you think so little of my sister that you would write something as offensive . . . as disgusting as this?" He crumbled the note into his fist and shook it at Gavin.

"No . . . wait, let me explain."

"Explain why I should not kill you right now."

Michael came to stand by Colin, looking just as befuddled. "What did it say?"

"Nothing I can repeat aloud." He took a step toward Gavin. "You have not only lost your memory, you have lost your mind!"

"I did not write the note!" Gavin said, holding up one hand in his defense while the other hand clutched the box.

"You deny that this is for Diana?"

"No, but it is not from me." He took a deep breath. "I did not want to tell you this before, because you know how Diana is. She would not want your interference."

"My interference?" Colin looked ready to explode. "You better get to the point quickly, Tamesly. I am running out of patience."

"Diana has an admirer of sorts. He has been sending her roses. I caught a young lad dropping off this box earlier today on her front step. That is where I was coming from when you met me, Colin. I decided to take the box and examine the contents here. I want to find out who has been sending her these flowers." He stepped toward Colin. "I swear that is the truth. You have to believe me. I cherish Diana. I *love* her. I would never do anything to upset her in any way."

Colin stared him down for a moment, then relaxed a tiny bit. "It did not seem like something you would say," he finally responded.

"May I?" Gavin held out his hand for the note. Colin handed it to him in silence. When Gavin read the words on the paper, his stomach lurched. What had started as a sweet, romantic poem dissolved into a paragraph of lewd descriptions that weren't fit for anyone's eyes, especially someone as well-bred as Diana.

No wonder Colin had been furious with him.

"Tell me about these roses," Michael asked, taking the box from Gavin as if he had a right to it.

"They were different colors. Purple, pink, orange, and now red." Gavin looked at the rose lying in the box.

"Lavender," Michael said, picking up the rose and examining it.

"No, red," Gavin corrected.

The man gave Gavin a half-smile. "I know this one

is red, but the first one must have been lavender. A light purple. Correct?"

"How did you know that?"

"The colors, they each have a meaning. Lavender is for attraction, pink for admiration, orange for passion, red for love."

"I didn't know you had such a knowledge of flowers," Gavin remarked.

"It is my business to know lots of things."

"So what does it all mean?" Gavin was running out of patience. The note had unnerved him more than he was letting on. That someone would write something so vulgar to Diana . . . he wanted to wring the man's neck.

"I am not sure," Michael said.

"Right now we need to figure out who this cretin is," Colin added, his anger down to a simmer, but palpable nevertheless.

"There is nothing else in the box," Michael said, examining the container. "Nothing but the flower and the packaging."

Gavin looked at the note in his hand. He was loath to read it again, but he had to make sure he hadn't missed anything. As he studied it he suddenly said, "Wait . . . there is something different here. Other than the content."

"What?" Michael asked.

"The handwriting . . . it is not the same as the other notes." He walked over to his desk, opened the top drawer, and retrieved the note he'd taken from Diana the day before. "This one is definitely different."

Michael and Colin looked at the two notes, and nodded their agreement. Gavin took the note that had accompanied the red rose and examined it closely. "Bloody . . ."

"Gavin?" Colin asked.

"I recognize this handwriting." Images of numbers and names swam in his mind. He'd seen these slanted letters time and time again on the ledgers he'd studied over the past weeks.

"Gav? Do you remember something?" Colin asked.

"Yes," Gavin said slowly.

Colin clasped him on the shoulder. "Your memory has returned?"

"No . . . not that." He looked at Colin and Michael. "We have to get to Diana. I know who wrote this note."

"Who?" both men asked simultaneously.

"My cousin. I do not know what he is up to, but I do know Diana is in danger."

"You sent me the roses?" Diana's hand flew to her chest in shock.

"You seem surprised." Percival walked toward her. He reeked of alcohol, but his steps were steady and sure, hardly the stance of a drunkard. "I suppose you thought my addled cousin had given them to you. He is, after all, a romantic slop of a gent."

"He is not addled," she insisted. Gooseflesh stood up on her arms.

"He cannot remember anything," Percival sneered. "That is the definition of addled to me." His gaze raked over Diana in one slow, lingering motion. "I can see why he could never forget you. Did you get my last gift? His eyes were glazed with desire. "I cannot wait to do all the things to you I wrote about."

She had no idea what he was talking about, nor did she care. Gooseflesh stood up on her arms. The man made her skin crawl. "Leave," she said, bringing her other arm across her chest in an unknowing attempt to shield herself from his leering stare.

"I do not think so." His tone dripped with confidence. "I am quite comfortable right here."

"I will have Davies throw you out."

Percival clucked his tongue. "That will not be possible. Your late husband made a poor choice in servants, you see. Davies is quite the weakling when caught unawares."

Diana gasped. "What did you do to him?"

"Oh, he is still alive. Unconscious, but alive."

She wanted to ask about Honor, but refrained. She prayed her maid had somehow gone into hiding, or had at least escaped and was seeking help.

"Now that we are alone," Percival said, "we will not be interrupted."

His meaning was perfectly clear. She forced her

voice not to shake. Showing her fear would be a colossal mistake, and she'd made enough of those lately. "You will not get away with this."

He reached and yanked out the clip that held her hair in place. He let the strands fall through his fingers. "So soft. Just as I imagined." He gazed at her with drunken eyes. "I hope the rest of is just as I imagined too."

Bile crawled up her throat. She stepped backward, but he matched her movements until she was pressed against the wall. Tears flooded her eyes. "Do not do this," she whispered, her voice thick.

"Is that begging I hear?" He leaned in close and pressed his mouth against her ear. "Beg some more."

Diana shut her eyes tight. This nightmare couldn't be happening. She cursed her insistence on being independent, thinking she would be safe with her butler and her maid. Now she had no idea where they were or how seriously they were hurt. And she had no idea how she would fight against Percival. But she had to at least try. Pressing her arms against his chest, she shoved as hard as she could.

Staggering backward, he fell against the sideboard, hitting his head on the corner of the massive piece of furniture. Blood poured from the wound on his head as he crumpled to the floor. Not waiting to see if he was conscious, she fled the room and ran to the foyer. Her hand touched the doorknob.

She felt someone grip the back of her dress and

yank her from the door. She was flung around until she faced Percival. A rivulet of blood flowed down his cheek, mixing in with his sweat.

"You will pay for that," he growled. "You will pay dearly for that."

Chapter Seventeen

Gavin, Colin, and Michael had taken Michael's plush coach to Diana's house. She was a mere ten minutes away, but to Gavin it felt like an eternity.

He could only imagine what nefarious plan Percival had for Diana. Hopefully he hadn't had time to enact it. But a feeling deep in his gut told him that they might be too late.

"Can your driver not go faster?" Gavin stamped his foot on the floor of the coach.

"He is going as fast as he can," Michael responded calmly.

Gavin looked across at him, then at Colin, who also appeared calm. He would have thought his friend had no reaction to what was going on, except he saw that

Colin's hands were clenched. The man was barely keeping his nerves contained.

Gavin wished he could be so self-composed.

Finally the coach skidded to a stop, and the men poured out. Light flooded out of two windows, one of which was Diana's sitting room. He ran ahead of Michael and Colin and reached the front step in record time. The door was ajar. He burst into the house.

A woman's scream pierced his eardrums.

"Scream all you like, darling," Percival said through gritted teeth. He had a hold of Diana's hair and yanked it again. "The louder the better."

She clamped her lips tightly, tears streaming down her cheeks from the pain. She wouldn't give him the satisfaction of pleasing him. "You are a vile, evil man," she ground out.

"And you, my dear, are easy prey."

Suddenly he let go of her. Then she realized he hadn't released her on his own volition. He had been tackled to the ground by a taller man, who was plowing his fists into Percival's face.

"Diana!" Colin came up to her. He put his arm around her shoulders. "Are you all right?"

She leaned against her brother, grateful for his support. Her legs felt like gelatin. "I—I think so." Watching the men fight on the floor of her sitting room, she realized who her rescuer was.

Gavin.

Percival scrambled out from beneath Gavin's hold. He stood and punched Gavin in the gut, then kicked him in the head. Unfazed, Gavin leapt to his feet and rammed his shoulder into his cousin's chest. Then another man entered the fray. Her mouth dropped open in shock as Michael grabbed Percival from behind and held him taut.

"Gavin!" Colin shouted. "Enough!"

But Gavin either didn't hear him or ignored his words. He continued to flail until Michael dragged Percival away.

Doubled over and heaving for air, Gavin lifted his head to look at Diana. When was finally able to stand, she ran into his arms.

"Thank God you came," she said, burying her head into his chest. She melted against him as his arms went around her shoulders. She felt him rest his cheek against the top of her head. "I—I do not know what I would have done . . ."

"Shh," he said, still breathing heavily. "You do not have to find out."

She heard footsteps come up behind her. "Michael has him subdued," Colin said. "You gave him quite a beating."

"Not as much as he deserved," Gavin remarked.

"Michael is taking him to the authorities. I will accompany him and make sure Percival does not cause any more trouble." Diana felt her brother's hand on her shoulder. "Thank God we got here in time. Will you be all right? Shall I get mother?"

"No," she said, but her voice still trembled. "There is no need to worry her."

"Are you sure?"

"I will be fine." She gazed up at Gavin, taking in his bruised and bloody face. Percival had gotten in more than a few blows.

"All right." Colin looked at Gavin and shook his head. "Better get a doctor to look at that."

"I will have Seamus tend to it."

Diana suddenly remembered Davies and Honor. She left Gavin's arms and went to Colin. "You must find them," she pleaded after she explained what happened.

"I will. Do not worry." He tilted his head in Gavin's direction. "Take care of him first." Then he dashed out of the room.

Diana took his hand, feeling the scrapes against his knuckles. Scrapes he had incurred on her behalf. "You should sit down," she said, focusing all her energy into taking care of him.

He shook his head. "I am all bloody. Your furniture—"

"It does not matter." She led him to the sofa and made him sit down. She lowered her body next to him, then withdrew a handkerchief from the inside cuff of her sleeve and started dabbing at the blood on his lip. "When will you understand that the only thing I care about is you?"

"I guess it just takes some getting used to." Suddenly he brought his hands to his head. "Oh . . . that hurts!"

"Gavin?" She watched helplessly as he bent over, his palms gripping the sides of his head. He howled in pain. "Gavin . . . what is it? What is wrong?"

The ache in his head was excruciating. It had come on without warning, and now it threatened to take him out. Nausea gripped him, and he prayed he wouldn't throw up. "Pain . . ." he managed to say.

"What can I do for you?" Diana knelt beside him, her hand resting on his knee.

At any other moment he would have enjoyed the close contact, but right now he barely noticed her there. "Seamus . . ." he uttered as the room turned upside down. A final stab of pain sliced through his head.

Then everything went black.

Diana stood by the window in her sitting room, staring out into the darkness. Her arms were crossed over her chest, and she leaned against the window frame. She should be exhausted, but every nerve in her body was strung tight. She wouldn't relax until she learned if Gavin would be all right.

The night's events ran through her mind in a hazy

torrent. After Gavin had passed out, Colin had appeared, having found Davies and Honor. They had been knocked unconscious, but would be all right. Colin then fetched Seamus, who had arrived posthaste. He and Colin had helped Gavin to Diana's guest room, where Seamus was tending to him at the moment. During all of this Michael had transported Percival to the authorities.

A tremor passed through her, although she wasn't cold. She didn't know what she would have done if Gavin hadn't shown up. She was also indebted to her brother and Michael, but in her eyes Gavin was her hero.

He had to be all right. He just had to be.

"Looks like you've had a rough night of it, lassie."

Diana whirled around at the sound of Seamus's voice. She left her post at the window and went to him. "Gavin?"

"He is resting. I gave him something for the pain. Oddest thing, said it came up on him all of the sudden. Though, he did take quite a blow in the head from Percy."

"More than one blow," Diana corrected.

"Aye, that he did."

"Will he be all right?"

"I believe so."

Panic wound through her. "But you are not sure?"

He gave her a gentle look. "Listen, lass, if there is one thing I have learned is that head injuries are unpredictable. He has already had a severe one. I cannot tell if the blows he took aggravated his condition, not until he has had some time to rest. But I can tell you this . . ." he took her hand. "Gavin is a tough lad."

Diana swallowed her anxiety. "May I see him?"

"Of course. I recommend it."

A few moments later she crept into the room, not wanting to disturb him. She had never been in this room very often, as she had very few overnight guests. It had a musty, unused smell, and she immediately regretted that Gavin had to convalesce here. He deserved so much better.

Quietly she went to the chair that had been pulled near the bed and sat down. He lay underneath the coverlet, and she could see that Seamus had pulled off his shirt, which had been stained with blood. A dark bruise was already forming on his bare shoulder. Her gaze went to his face, swollen and purple-hued, Seamus obviously having cleaned up the cuts. His eyes were closed, his long, thick lashes lying against the uppermost part of his cheeks.

Her heart squeezed inside her chest. More than anything she wanted to climb in next to him, to put her arms around him, to feel his heart beat against her cheek. Before she could stop them, tears slid down her cheeks, one landing on his hand.

His eyes fluttered open. "Diana," he whispered, his lips curving into a small smile.

She could tell the movement caused him pain. "Shhh," she said, wiping her tears off his hand, then entwining her fingers with his. "Go back to sleep."

"I was not asleep," he said, squeezing her fingers lightly. "I am glad you are here." His eyes closed again. "Now . . . I can sleep."

Diana held on to his hand until she saw his chest rise and fall in a slow, steady rhythm. She brought his hand to her lips and pressed her mouth against his skin. "I love you," she whispered. "I love you so much."

Gavin's eyes were sticky and dry when he opened them. He turned his head, relieved that the pain wasn't so severe. He remembered Seamus giving him something, and silently thanked his friend for coming to his rescue. He continued to look around the room, and saw the sunlight streaming in through the beige curtains that draped across the window.

Then he became aware of the small, delicate hand gripping his. He glanced at her, asleep in the chair, her chin resting on her chest. He smiled. She had stayed here with him all night. No wonder he had slept so peacefully. He lifted up his hand and looked at her slender fingers, the nails beautifully buffed and shaped into round ovals. Everything about Diana was perfect. And she was finally his.

His eyes widened. *Finally* his? Where had that come from?

"Gavin?" Diana lifted her head, her eyes opening slowly. She looked at their hands joined together, then smiled.

"Good morning," he said softly.

"Good morning."

"Thank you for staying with me."

She leaned forward, her hand still clasping his. "No, it is I who must thank you. You saved me from your dreadful cousin."

Gavin grit his teeth. "I could have killed him."

"You almost did, if Michael had not pulled him away from you."

He lifted his head and searched her face. "He did not do anything to you, did he?"

She shook her head. "No. Nothing like that."

"Thank God . . ." He suddenly gasped. The pain had returned. He let go of her hand and gripped his head.

"Gavin? You want I should fetch Seamus?"

He nodded, and she flew out of the room.

Seconds later Seamus arrived, appearing disheveled, as if he had slept on the sofa all night. Knowing his friend, he probably did. "Hurts, does it lad?"

"Yes," he responded with a half gasp.

"Can you do something for him?" Diana asked, panic tinging her voice.

"I can give him more laudanum," Seamus said. "But I do not want to give him too much."

The pain intensified, making Gavin desperate. "Just give me the medicine," he begged.

Seamus administered the laudanum, and shortly thereafter the pain subsided, but the groggy side effect also kicked in. "What is happening?" he asked Seamus, his voice sounding slightly slurred.

For the first time that Gavin could remember, his old friend looked worried. "I do not know lad," he said. "I do not know."

Chapter Eighteen

"What do you mean, you do not know?" Diana asked as soon as Gavin had fallen asleep. "You are a doctor; you are supposed to know what is wrong! You are supposed to heal him!"

"Quiet, lass," Seamus admonished. "Do you want him to hear you? If you want to berate me in such a fashion, let us at least get out of his earshot."

Diana wilted against the chair. "I am sorry. I do not mean to take out my frustration on you, Seamus."

"I understand." He moved toward the door and gestured she follow him. "Come," he said.

When they were in her sitting room, he motioned for her to sit down. His bushy brows furrowed. "Just because I do not understand his symptoms does not mean I cannot help him. I will do everything in my power to figure out what is wrong."

"I know." She stared down at her hands, which were resting in her lap. "Again, I am sorry. It is just that I am so worried."

"I know you are. I am too. I am just not supposed to admit it." He tugged on his stubbled chin. "He needs to come back home, but I do not want to move him just yet, not until he can maintain consciousness for a short period without pain."

Diana nodded. "He can stay here as long as he wishes. I will take care of him."

"I never doubted that for a moment. But I do not think you should bear this burden alone."

"You do not think . . . oh, Seamus, I could not bear to lose him."

He patted her hand. "No, I do not think it is nearly that dire, lass. Let me ask Elizabeth to come help."

Diana shook her head. "I do not want my mother to know about this."

"Why? Are you really that independent? Are you that proud that you will not accept help?"

Her posture slumped slightly. "No, it is not that. I just do not want her to worry."

"She worries no matter what, lass. That is what mothers do."

"I know." She took a deep breath, knowing she could

really use her mother's help and support. "All right. But I refuse to leave him alone."

"I will be happy to fetch her," he said, rising from the sofa.

Despite her worry over Gavin, she couldn't help but smile. "I am sure you would."

Seamus returned her grin. "Try not to fret too much, Diana. Be strong for him. He needs that right now."

She nodded. "I will. I promise you that."

When Seamus left, Diana checked on Gavin. He was sleeping soundly, and she didn't want to disturb him. Her stomach growled, and she realized she hadn't had anything to eat. She headed to the kitchen to fix herself a snack. Seamus had told her to be strong. It wouldn't do for her to be lightheaded from hunger.

After preparing a small sandwich with cold beef and cheddar cheese, she poured herself a glass of milk and sat down at the kitchen table. The food didn't look appetizing and it tasted bland, but at least it was nourishment. She had been so focused on Gavin that she hadn't had a thought for her loyal maid and butler. Vowing to see if they were in the house, she quickly tucked into her sparse meal and dealt with the fresh wave of guilt that overcame her. For once again, she had been the source of someone's pain. This time not only the man she loved, but the servants who had been taken care of her all these years.

She had just eaten the last morsel when Colin appeared in the doorway, looking as weary and worn out as she felt. Standing up, she met Colin halfway and fell into his embrace, grateful for his strength. Never had her brother come through for her like he had yesterday.

"How are you holding up?" he asked as she took a step backward to look up at him.

"I have had better times." She gave him a trembling smile. "Thank you for being there for me. You are a prime brother, you know that?"

"Of course I am," he said, his mouth quirking into a tired half-smile. "I am just glad Gavin figured out it was Percival sending you the roses." His countenance grew stern. "Diana, why did you not say anything to me about that?"

"To be honest, Colin, at first I thought Gavin had sent the flowers." She looked away, embarrassed at having to admit her presumptuousness. "Then when I discovered he did not, I tried to put it out of my mind. I truly I did not want to bother you with it."

He moved away from her and ran his hand through his blond hair, frustration coloring his features. "Diana, when will you understand that you are never a bother to any of us? I should have insisted you move in with mother after William died. Or you could have stayed with Lily and me."

She tilted up her chin. "I would have refused."

"Yes, I suppose you would have. You are quite the stubborn woman." He sighed. "How is the patient?"

"Sleeping. He had another horrible headache. Seamus gave him some more laudanum, but he cannot keep taking it. Even I know that." She lowered her voice. "I am worried about him, Colin."

"We all are."

"I do not know what I will do if he does not recover from this." Her voice was laced with emotion.

"I do not think you have to worry about that, Diana. Gavin is a fighter, and he will fight through this. I have to admit, though, he surprised me. I had never seen him so enraged before. When he saw what that jack o' knapes was doing to you, he seemed to lose all reason."

Diana shuddered. "Percival Parringer is truly an evil man." Speaking of Percival reminded her of her servants. "Do you know what happened to Davies and Honor? I have not seen them at all today. Please tell me they are all right."

"They were both hit over the head and knocked unconscious, but they will be fine. Honor is with Lily right now, and Davies is staying with his brother. He has a rather nasty bump on the back of the head. He is lucky Percival did not kill him."

Relief flowed through her. "I am glad they are all right." She sighed and sat down at the table. "And what of Percival?"

"That lout is in custody. Michael made sure of it. Trust me, Diana. Percival Parringer will never bother you or anyone else ever again."

"I did not realize Michael had that much influence."

Colin glanced away for a moment. "Michael is full of surprises."

"He always has been," she replied. She looked at the crusty leftovers of her sandwich. "Can I fix you something to eat? It will not be a huge meal, but I can put together something light."

"No thank you, I am not hungry. I just stopped by to check on you and Gavin, and to tell you that I am insisting you move in with Lily and me immediately."

"I cannot do that."

"Diana, now is not the time to be stubborn."

"You said Percival was in custody. The danger is over."

"That may be the case, but I still think—"

"I spoke with Seamus this morning. He is bringing Mother over this afternoon, and she will help me with Gavin. I imagine he will be staying as well. Therefore, I will not be alone. Does that make you feel better?"

"It does . . . a little." Colin regarded her for a moment. "I will send over Hughes to temporarily relieve Davies. And I am sure Lily can part with her maid for a few days until Honor is ready to return."

"But what will you do?"

He chuckled. "Diana, I do believe we can manage quite well without servants for a short time. I will also send a personal guard to keep an eye on things here."

She opened her mouth to argue, but knew it would be pointless. Besides, she was grateful for his intervention. With her family's help she would be able to devote all her attention to Gavin.

"Diana?" Colin reached for her hand. "You've gone pale all of the sudden. What is it?"

"It is nothing. I think I am tired. I slept in the chair all night."

"When Mother arrives you should try to get some sleep. In a bed this time," he said pointedly.

She nodded. "Yes, my lord," she said in a teasing tone. Then she paused. "Colin, do you really think Percival is out of our lives for good?"

He nodded. "Considering what he did to you and Gavin, he will be in gaol for a very long time."

Letting out a sigh of relief she said, "Good. I do not know what I would do if I saw him again."

"You do not ever have to find out."

She hoped he was right.

A cloudy haze surrounded him in all directions as images danced all around him. People he had never met, but thought he should know. Places he'd been to, but didn't recognize. Family members he had loved, but felt nothing for now.

His head pounded as he spun around in a circle. Never had he experienced such pain. The images whirled faster as they closed in on him. Everything became a blur. Suddenly he realized what the mass of mental pictures were.

They were his life.

The agony in his head intensified until he thought he would explode. He fell to his knees and cried out, but heard no sound. What was happening to him? Was he dying? Or was he going insane?

Then everything stopped. He saw nothing, heard nothing, felt nothing. Total darkness enveloped him. He welcomed the numbing blankness. Anything was better than the acute pain that had assaulted him.

A dim light appeared, then brightened. He heard a sweet feminine voice call his name.

"Gavin? Gavin?"

Gavin opened his eyes to the vision standing over him. Diana. She was so beautiful, even with the worried expression on her face. Unable to help himself, he cupped her cheek with his hand. Then he caught sight of his forearm, shiny and slick with sweat. He suddenly realized his body was drenched.

She covered his hand with her own. "Can you hear me, Gavin?"

He nodded.

Relief passed across her features. "Thank God. I have been calling your name for the last fifteen minutes. I was about to fetch Seamus when you woke up." She released his hand and stepped away for a moment. When she returned she had a dry cloth and proceeded to dab at his forehead and cheeks with it, mopping up the perspiration that had gathered there.

When he started to speak, he discovered his mouth

was dry. "Thirsty," he managed to say, feeling weak and drained, but thinking he had the best nursemaid in the world.

"Here." She held a cup to his lips and he drank from it.

"Thanks." He leaned back on the pillow. "What happened?"

"You mean you don't know?" Anxiety crept up on her face again. "Your cousin . . . he did terrible things . . . you rescued me . . ."

"No, love," he said softly. "I remember all that, unfortunately. What happened while I was asleep?"

"You were thrashing about on the bed, having a terrible time. As if you were having a nightmare."

"I was."

A pained expression crossed her lovely features. "I am so sorry about that. How is your head? Does it still hurt?"

"No," he said, already feeling stronger. "Surprisingly not. Actually, other than being tired and a few body aches, I feel fine."

A smile lit up her face. "Truly?"

"Truly. In fact, I think I should sit up."

"Slowly," she warned. Then she put her arm behind his shoulders to assist him.

He breathed in the heady scent of her perfumed skin. A lock of her silky blond hair fell across his chest as she helped him to a seated position. He turned to look at her, their faces only inches apart. Finding he could stand it no longer, he captured her mouth with his own.

Her hesitation showed he'd caught her off guard, but she paused for less than a second before returning his kiss. The contact was as sweet, yet as fiery, as he'd imagined. He couldn't believe he was kissing the most precious, most beautiful woman in London. No, not just in London, or even England for that matter. In the world. Yet here he was, cupping her face with his hands, kissing her with all the pent up longing he'd felt for what seemed a lifetime.

When they finally parted, her eyes glistened with tears, piercing him in the heart. He immediately regretted his rashness. "I am so sorry . . . I could not resist . . . I should not have taken advantage of you—"

Her mouth covered his again in a kiss more passionate than the first. She broke the contact and said, "Now who is taking advantage of whom?"

He grinned and wiped her tears with the pads of his thumbs. "Then why are you crying?"

"Tears of happiness, you dolt!" She sat down on the edge of the bed and faced him. "I am so happy! I never thought I would feel this way, Gavin. I never thought I would love someone like I love you."

"You love me?"

"Do not act so surprised," she said with a grin.

"No, it is just that I love hearing it. I love you too." Pulling her against him he kissed her again, not ever wanting to let her go.

But he had to. They could not go on kissing like this without it leading to more. He had vowed to never take advantage of her, and he would keep that promise. "We must stop," he said, whispering against her lips.

She pulled back slowly, the disappointment in her eyes nearly undoing his resolve. "I know," she said, moving off the bed and back to the chair. A safe distance for both of them, but to him it felt like a chasm had suddenly opened up between them.

Seamus then strode into the room, and Gavin was thankful they had separated when they did. Although from the way the older man looked from him to Diana and then back again, Gavin suspected he knew exactly what they had being doing moments before.

"I take it you are feeling better?" Seamus said, giving Gavin a knowing look as he neared his bedside.

"Yes," Gavin simply said. No need to elaborate or embarrass Diana.

"Good." Seamus gently lifted one of Gavin's eyelids, then the other. "Any pain?"

Gavin shook his head. "No. Not a bit. Seems to have disappeared."

"You have been sweating," Seamus said, moving back a few steps. "Do you feel feverish?"

"No. I had some kind of nightmare."

"He grew quite violent," Diana added, rising from her chair. "I was just leaving to get you, but then he awakened."

"And you did not want to leave him alone, did you lass?" Seamus winked at her.

"I, well, no—"

"Leave her be, Seamus," Gavin snapped, irritated at his friend for teasing her. The last thing he wanted was for her to feel uncomfortable.

"Aye, I was just having a bit o' fun." He smiled at Diana. "You have had a remarkable healing effect on the lad, I must say. If he continues like this, I think he will be ready to go home in a couple of days."

Gavin thought he saw a flicker of disappointment flash across her cerulean eyes. "That would be fantastic," she said, sounding less enthusiastic than her words would imply.

"I should let Elizabeth know the good news. You still need your rest, Gavin. Do not overexert yourself." He gave him a stern look.

Gavin comprehended his meaning immediately. "Understood."

After Seamus left, an awkward silence fell between Gavin and Diana. A hint of sadness was evident in her expression. "Is there something wrong?" he asked, concerned.

"I am just being silly," she said, averting her gaze.

"Tell me. I promise not to think you are silly."

She looked at him directly. "I am glad you are feeling better, I really am. But I . . . I will miss you." Exhaling a breath, she said, "There. I admitted it. You must think I am behaving like a besotted school girl."

Actually, he thought she was the most wonderful woman in the world. His heart filled with love for her. "I do not think that is silly at all. I feel the same way."

"You do?"

He nodded. "And I think I know of a way we can rectify the situation."

"How?"

Inhaling a deep breath, he took the plunge. "Diana, will you—"

His words were cut off as a pain worse than any he had felt prior seared his mind, blinding him in a haze of white-hot agony. Diana called his name, her voice sounding small and far away. He cradled his head in his hands, as if that would assuage the torturous aching. Then just as suddenly, it disappeared, and everything came back in focus.

Everything.

Chapter Nineteen

The memories came flooding back with a ferocity that nearly stole the breath from his body.

"Gavin?" She gripped his hand, her blue eyes stark with fear. An overabundance of emotions overcame him as he stared at her, trying to reconcile the past with the present.

Oh, how he had loved her. The pain of her rejection came back with stabbing force. He remembered the last time they had been together before he'd left for India. She told him she never wanted to see him ever again with such venom and hate he never thought he would have survived it. And of course, loving her as much as he did, he obliged. She had wanted him gone, and he left.

Glancing down at her hand in his, he wondered

what game she was playing now. Her declarations of love now rang false in his ears. She couldn't have suddenly sprouted feelings for him in the past few weeks, not when she had held him in such poor favor so long ago. He released her fingers as if they were red-hot.

"Gavin?" she asked, the fear in her eyes mixing with uneasiness. "What is happening?"

"I remember," he said bluntly, unable to look at her anymore. "I remember everything."

Ice flowed through Diana's veins as she heard Gavin's words and saw his accompanying expression. Instead of exulting in finally regaining his memory, he remained quiet, his gaze averted, a scowl forming on his face. Her stomach twisted into a knot. Dear Lord, he couldn't even look at her. He really did remember everything.

Gathering up her courage, she pasted a smile on her face, trying to diffuse the tension. "Your memory has returned?"

"Yes," he said flatly.

"That's . . ." she swallowed the lump that had suddenly congealed in her throat. "That's wonderful, Gavin."

He finally turned to her, his green eyes flinty stones. "You think so? Or is that simply part of your act?"

"Act? Gavin, I do not understand what you mean."

"Do not play coy, Diana. It might have worked

when you were a young ingénue, but now it does not become you."

His words cut her to the quick. "Gavin, you have to believe me. I am not putting on an 'act' as you call it."

"Oh, really? Then what is your game, Diana? For surely you have one. You always do."

"Gavin, please." Tears burned in her eyes. Blast, she did not want to melt into a puddle of sobs, not when he was looking at her with such coldness. She reached for his hand, and while he didn't pull away, he didn't grip her fingers either. "I was afraid this was going to happen."

"What? That I would remember how you treated me? How you pretended to like me, pretended that we had a chance together, only to turn around and marry someone else? And when I tried to warn you against him, you dismissed me like a pesky fly. Were those the memories you hoped to resurrect?" His eyes narrowed. "Or were you hoping I would never remember them at all?"

Diana didn't know what to say. How could she defend herself when she had no defense? Then she knew what she had to do. It would require her to swallow her pride, to lay her feelings bare. Something he had done so many years ago when he had pledged his love, when he had cared enough for her that even after her rejection, he had tried to protect her.

She got down on her knees and took his hand in both of hers. Laying her forehead on top of the back of his hand, she said, "I know I do not deserve it . . . but please forgive me."

Gavin fought a desperate war within himself. Outwardly he remained stock still, his hand lying limply in hers, trying to ignore the warmth of her skin against his. Yet he was quaking inside, the trembling threatening to overtake him. She was begging for his forgiveness. Literally begging. The most beautiful woman in London, the one who had discarded men with little care for their feelings, who had trampled on his own emotions until they were raw and bleeding, was on her knees.

He didn't know what to say. What to think. What to *feel.*

Then he felt her tears on his skin, heard her muffled sobs, and the ice that had crystallized around his heart thawed.

Lifting up her head, she gazed at him, her eyes awash in tears. "You were right about William, Gavin. I should have listened to you. But I was stupid. And proud. And vain. I did not want to admit that I made a mistake. That out of all the men that . . . that had wanted me, I chose unwisely." Her lips trembled. "I chose him over you."

"Diana," he whispered, closing his eyes against the pain. His pain . . . and hers.

"No, I need to say this. You need to hear it. William betrayed me, as I am sure you knew he would. He was always discreet with his dalliances, but he never missed a chance to rub it in my face. It was almost as if marrying me had been a personal conquest. And once he had won me over . . . he had no use for me.

"One day four years ago he came home late, probably from another one of his mistresses. He had a cough, and at that time I did not care about how he felt. But then his health declined quickly, and he died from consumption. And you know what? I never shed a tear over his passing. My family thought I was in shock, as they thought we had a wonderful marriage. I had kept up the charade for them. I did not want anyone to know my shame."

He slipped his hand out from her grip and wiped her tears with his thumb, unable to help himself. "You did not deserve that," he said.

"But I did! Do you not see, Gavin? I deserved to be treated as I had treated everyone else. Maybe that had been William's plan all along. Do you know what your cousin said to me that night at my brother's party?"

"Diana, you do not have to tell me."

She ignored him. "He said I thought I was too good for him. And he was right. I always thought I was too good for everyone. It was all a game to me. But the great Diana Dymoke finally got a taste of her own bitter medicine. And all I could think about was how I should have listened to you. How much you had cared for me. After awhile, I had to put you out of my mind. I could not bear to remember what I had lost."

"Why did you not tell me these things before?"

"Perhaps I should have. But when you returned, it was as if I could start all over. I wanted to help you regain your memories, to redeem myself for what I had done to you. But then . . . I fell in love with you."

He closed his eyes again, trying to sort his jumbled emotions.

After a long moment, she spoke. "Gavin?"

Opening his eyes, he turned to her. "I want to believe you, Diana. But I do not know if I can."

Diana thought it would have been less painful if Gavin had driven a dagger into her breast than to see the look of distrust in his eyes. When he had wiped away her tears, she thought maybe they had a chance after all, that her confession had repaired the damage of the past. But it had been a false hope. He had given her his pity, not his love. She had killed that love long ago.

"I need to be alone," he said, staring down at the bedclothes that covered him from his feet to the middle of his torso.

She nodded and rose from her knees, then straightened her skirts and wiped her cheeks with her fingers. She tried to stem the sobs that collected in her chest and threatened to escape and embarrass them both. "This is good-bye, then?"

His eyes remained transfixed in front of him. "I suppose so."

Turning to flee, she stopped herself. Spinning back around, she grabbed Gavin's face in both her hands and kissed him hard and long, forcing her love for him to travel from her lips to his, willing him to understand the truth that resided in her heart. When they parted, he gave her a quick glance, then averted his gaze once again.

Unable to keep her tears at bay any longer, she ran out of the room, nearly slamming into Seamus. "Lass, what is it?"

She looked at the kind doctor who would soon be her stepfather. "Gavin . . . he has . . ."

"What, Diana? What has happened to Gavin?"

"He remembers." With that, she dashed away.

"Bloody hell, lad, what did you do to her?"

Gavin gave Seamus a black look. "Nothing. I did nothing to her except remember what she did to me."

Seamus's eyes grew wide. "So it is true? You have regained your memory!" He strode toward Gavin and embraced him in a hug, clapping him on the back. "Oh lad, I cannot tell you how happy that makes me!" He pulled back, his grin wide and infectious. "I have been waitin' to ask you this question for eight years. What were you doing on the docks of Calcutta?"

Leaning back against his pillow, he mined his memories, able to recall everything. It was as if he'd never had amnesia at all. "I went to speak to Diana, to warn her against William," he said. "When she turned me away, I left the country. I only meant to be gone a couple of months, to sort out my feelings." He sighed. "I really left to try to forget her."

"You certainly did a bang-up job of that," Seamus said, letting out a chuckle. "Oh come lad, 'tis a small joke."

"It's not amusing."

Seamus sobered. "Sorry. Please, continue."

"When I disembarked off the ship, I was approached by four men, not of Indian descent. They appeared to be English, but spoke in a foreign tongue. At first I thought they were there to help me with my bags. Foolish and silly of me, now that I look back on it. The next thing I knew they had me by the arms and forced me into an alley."

"Didn't anyone see them drag you away?"

"The docks were so crowded. These blokes were skilled. I am sure anyone watching thought they were escorting me somewhere. Once they got me into the alley, they started to beat me. After a few well-placed blows, I lost consciousness. The next thing I knew I was waking up in your clinic . . . and you know the rest."

Seamus let out a low whistle. "I am so sorry lad, for what happened." He gave Gavin a fatherly pat on the forearm, then grinned. "But buck up! You have your memories back, and the woman you love. You should be celebratin'."

Except that Gavin wasn't in the mood to celebrate. He wondered if he would be ever again.

Seamus's smile faded. "All right, Gavin. Out with it. You should be tap dancin' on the bed here, not stewin' in your own juices like an overcooked pot roast."

At the mention of food, Gavin's stomach rumbled, but he ignored it. He had no appetite. The memories kept coming at him, like a barrage. His father and their mostly strained relationship. At least they had managed to reconcile shortly before his untimely death. The knowledge that Percival had been a pain in his backside for most of his life. Thankfully he had taken care of that problem once and for all. The memory of Colin's friendship, and how they had palled around in school and beyond, up until Colin had married Lily and Gavin had fallen in love with Diana.

Diana. The pain just kept lapping at his heart, like a wave on the shoreline. It tainted everything that had happened between them the past few weeks. He had felt pity for her when she had told him about William, but a small part of him also felt vindicated.

What kind of man was he, that he would exult in someone else's pain? Especially someone he had loved?

"Gavin? I say lad, are you with me?"

"I am here. I am just trying to sort all this out."

Seamus plopped down in the chair next to the bed. "For sure, it will take time for you to process all of this.

But that's no cause for you to be in such a dark mood. I think you are dealing with something more than your memories." He gave him a penetrating look. "Am I right?"

"Of course you are, and you know it." Gavin slumped in the bed. Just a few moments ago he had been kissing Diana, on the verge of proposing . . . then the memories returned.

And ruined everything.

"Diana seemed very upset when she left here," Seamus said quietly.

"I know."

"I am sure whatever has come between the two of you, it will work out in the end. You both love each other, any fool can see that."

Gavin looked at Seamus, a hopeless sensation flowing over him. "I am not sure that is enough."

Chapter Twenty

"Diana, darling," her mother cooed, holding her sobbing daughter in her arms. "Please, sweetheart. Tell me what is wrong. You said Gavin was all right."

"He is."

"Then why are you so upset?"

Sniffing, Diana wiped her damp handkerchief across her nose. She had hoped to avoid her mother and run upstairs to the privacy of her own bedroom, where she could nurse her wounds alone. But Elizabeth had been at the bottom of the stairwell when Diana reached it, and had immediately seen her daughter's distress. Now they were seated on the sofa in her sitting room, Diana trying not to go to pieces, yet doing exactly the opposite.

Elizabeth released her daughter and clasped Diana's

face in her hands. "This does have something to do with Gavin, does it not?"

Diana nodded.

"Darling, you know you can tell me anything. Of all my children, you have always been the one to keep your thoughts and feelings tucked tightly inside of you. But you do not have to do that, not anymore. I am here for you. I always have been."

"I know," she whispered thickly. "It is . . . it is just so hard . . ."

"Then start at the beginning."

And she did. She told her mother everything, from her first dance with Gavin so long ago to her travesty of a marriage to William, to her falling in love with Gavin upon his return, and then his remembrance of her rejection. By the time she was finished she was exhausted, but also relieved. The confession had been cathartic.

Elizabeth's expression was a blend of sympathy and irritation. "I had no idea about William," she said. "If I had, that man would have died well before his appointed time."

Diana couldn't help but smile. Her mother meant no such thing, but just having an ally made her feel better. "Please do not tell anyone else, especially Colin."

"It is none of his business. Do not worry, love. Everything you have told me will be kept in the strictest of confidence." She gave Diana an encouraging smile. "Now, what are you going to do about Gavin?"

"There is nothing to do," Diana said, twisting her

handkerchief into a knot. "I asked him to forgive me, and he told me to leave."

"Just like that?"

"Well, there was more to it than that," Diana admitted.

"I thought so. Tell me something. Do you still love him?"

"Of course."

Elizabeth took Diana's hand in hers. "Then listen to your heart, darling. It will tell you exactly what to do."

"Mama, that is far too cryptic an answer. Do you not have any other helpful advice?"

"No." She leaned forward and kissed her daughter on the cheek. "Other than to tell you to go upstairs and wash your face, change your dress, and get back in that room. Although I would call those motherly commands, not advice."

Diana wrinkled her nose. "I would too." She embraced her mother's slim shoulders. "Thank you, Mama," she said, close to tears once again. She didn't think she had any more left.

"You are welcome, darling. And do not worry. I have a feeling Gavin will come around soon. He has loved you for so very long, you know."

"I know. I just hope that it's enough."

"What do you mean you *hope* that love is enough?" Seamus bellowed. "Are you daft, lad? Of course it is enough. Love is everything!"

"Naturally you would say that," Gavin replied bitterly. "Being that you are completely besotted with Elizabeth and all that."

"True, I am a man in love," Seamus said. "But that does not mean I have taken leave of my senses, something you apparently have done."

"No, I have not." Gavin flung the covers off the bed and swung his legs over the side. He didn't want to spend another minute lying there, inactive. "Where is my shirt?"

"I tossed it. Did not think you wanted to wear a garment covered in your cousin's blood."

"Then what am I supposed to wear? I cannot walk around here without a shirt on!" Irritation rose within him. His head throbbed, but with a new type of pain. Tension. He could feel his muscles tightening all over. He wanted to leave this blasted room, this bloody house.

He had to escape.

Finding his boots laid neatly by the windowsill, he picked them up and jammed them on his feet. Seamus popped up from his chair.

"Where are you going, lad?"

"Anywhere but here."

"No, you are not. Doctor's orders."

"Then I relieve you from my care."

"For the love of—you will not step a foot out that door! Do you understand me?"

Gavin froze, staring at Seamus. The man had never

raised his voice before, even in anger, which was an extremely rare occurrence. But now he was yelling at him with such fervor his voice nearly shook the walls.

"Now that I have your attention," Seamus said, pointing to the chair he had just vacated, "you will sit. And you will keep your mouth shut and listen to what I have to say."

Mutely Gavin went to the chair and sat down, feeling like a child who had just been chastised for spilling his cup of milk. In a way Seamus's barking reminded him of his father.

Seamus cleared his throat, then began to pace back and forth in front of Gavin, his hands clasped behind his back. "I want you to understand that I know the reemergence of your memory is difficult to deal with. So some irritation on your part is to be expected."

"Some?" Gavin couldn't help remarking.

Seamus shot him a scathing look. "I did not give you permission to speak."

Gavin shrank back. "Sorry."

"Forgiven. Now, medically speaking, patients sufferin' from head trauma sometimes experience shifts in personality. From what I can gather, that has not happened to you. At least not until now. But I do not think that your behavior is due to a cracked head as much as it is a broken heart." Seamus stopped his pacing. "A condition, I might add, that you have the power to rectify."

"How? I am an idiot, Seamus. Not only did I fall in

love with a woman who did not love me in return, I fell in love with her twice."

"Yes, but she loves you back now."

"Oh, she thinks she does. But her feelings have a foundation of sand."

"Did she tell you this?"

"She does not have to. Right before I left for India, I warned her about the man she was about to marry. I had him investigated, without her knowledge. I discovered he was a rogue who had left a trail of women in his wake. The male version of Diana, so to speak."

"Ouch," Seamus said. "Do you not think that comment is rather harsh?"

"I suppose it is." Gavin slumped in the chair, feeling some of his ire drain out. "She told me she never wanted to see me again. So I obliged and left for India, and she married. What I did not know is that William had hurt her, more deeply than I had even thought he would." His words faded as he spoke them. Diana had certainly suffered.

"So you think she got her comeuppance?"

"No, I did not say that."

"But that is what you meant. Or what you hoped."

He looked at Seamus, discomfited by the disappointment he saw in the older man's face.

"I thought you were of stronger character than that," Seamus said quietly. "I guess I was wrong."

Gavin did not respond, lost in his own thoughts. He barely heard Seamus's footfalls as he headed for the door. He looked up when Seamus stopped just short of the doorway.

"Tell me somethin', lad. What if you had not left London?"

"What do you mean?"

"What if you had stayed? What if you had fought for her?" He stopped speaking for a moment. "Think about it. Is she worth fighting for now?" Turning on his heel, he left.

Gavin stared at the wall in front of him, doing as Seamus requested. What if he had never gone to India? He would have retained his memory, but that wasn't the point Seamus was making and he knew it. If he had stayed, if he had fought for Diana and won . . . she would have never married William. She would have never suffered the humiliation of being betrayed over and over again, of trying to hide a broken marriage from the outside world.

She had called him her hero. But he was no hero. He had failed her, yet she never blamed him. In fact, she had fallen in love with him despite it all.

The realization hit him straight on. Jumping up from his chair, he ran out of the room, oblivious to his state of undress. He headed straight for Diana's sitting room, hoping to find her there.

But the room was empty.

He traveled through the house, calling her name. She never answered.

Where had she gone? Finally Seamus appeared in

the foyer. Gavin gripped him by the shoulders, practically shaking the man with the ferocity of his emotion.

"Where is she? I have to talk to her."

"She left, lad. Went with Elizabeth. I imagine she will be stayin' there for quite awhile." He glanced around the room. "There cannot be any good memories here for her."

"That is true, Seamus. But with any luck she and I will make new memories together—and I guarantee you they will be good ones."

"That's the spirit!" Seamus laughed as Gavin headed out the door.

"What are you waiting for? We need to get to Elizabeth's posthaste. And what is so blasted funny?"

"You, lad." Seamus's jolly face beamed. "I do not think their butler will let you in with only your trousers on."

Gavin glanced down at his bare chest and grinned. "Guess we will be making a stop on the way there."

Chapter Twenty-one

Diana sat listlessly in front of the fireplace in the parlor of her mother's home. She had grown up here, and while the house held plenty of memories for her, it didn't feel like home. Neither did the flat she shared with William. She didn't belong anywhere. Not with her mother, and definitely not with Gavin.

The orange flames of the fire licked the blackened logs, emanating a warmth Diana couldn't feel. Her mother had told her to listen to her heart. She had been sitting there, staring at the fire, her mother's favorite shawl wrapped around her shoulders, trying to follow Elizabeth's advice. But her traitorous heart had remained silent.

All she felt was emptiness.

Her life was a shambles, and truly she had no one to

blame but herself. She had made all the choices that had led to this point, and now she was reaping the consequences. Alone.

Only when Gavin entered her thoughts did her emotions awaken, but the pain was too much to bear. With as much inner strength as she could muster, she compressed the ache deep inside her. Over time she knew she would heal, but she would never be the same again. If she had been damaged by William, allowing herself to love Gavin had wounded her even more.

"Diana?"

She turned at the sound of her mother's voice. "Yes?"

"You have a visitor."

Facing the fire again, she said, "I do not feel like seeing anyone right now. Please send them away."

"Are you sure?"

"Yes, Mama. I am sure."

She heard her mother sigh, then leave. Mesmerized by the fire, Diana continued to numb herself, trying to blank both her mind and heart. Her mother's advice had been useless.

The sound of heavy footsteps reached her ears. Assuming it was the butler, she continued to stare into the fireplace. It was teatime, and no doubt her mother would try to coerce her to eat whatever dry, bland food her cook Isabel had prepared for her. "Tell Mama I am not hungry," she said. "I know she will insist, but I cannot take in a single bite."

Gavin watched as Diana stared at the brightly burning fire in the hearth. Cocooned in a dark-red shawl, she seemed so tiny and fragile. When she had mistaken him for the butler, it had been on the tip of his tongue to say something witty or even a bit sarcastic. But words were not what was needed right now. He didn't need to speak to her.

He needed to act.

Silently he slipped off his boots, then crept on the soft carpeting in his stocking feet. So stealthily had he managed to move that she hadn't even noticed him coming right behind her. Her eyes were puffy and red, her cheeks hollow, her mouth drawn in an upside down half moon. The fire illuminated the sadness on her face, a sadness that touched him to his very soul.

She didn't deserve to suffer this way. She deserved to be loved, to be cherished. He had always thought that, ever since he had first laid eyes on her so long ago. That had never changed, despite the miles between them, despite the past. Gently, he placed his hands on her shoulders.

Gasping, she turned around and looked up at him. "Gavin?"

Without a word he knelt beside her, cupping the

back of her head with his hand. He drew her mouth to his and kissed her tenderly, exulting when she responded immediately. When he pulled away, he saw the moisture in her eyes through the haze of his own tears.

"Gavin, I—"

"Shh," he said, putting his finger on her lips. "Before you say anything, let me speak." He pressed his forehead against hers. "I am so very, very sorry."

Pulling away, she looked at him in surprise. "Why are you apologizing? You have nothing to be sorry for."

"Yes, I do." He blinked away the burning in his eyes. "I should have never left London."

"I know," she said. "I should have never driven you away."

He shook his head vehemently. "You do not understand. I should have never left you. I should have stayed and fought for you. If I had, you would have never married William."

Her mouth turned up slightly. "You do not know that. I was stubborn back then."

"Back then?" He smiled when she let out a small chuckle. He touched her face, rubbing his thumb across the top of her tearstained cheek. "I was selfish, Diana. I let my own ego get in the way of protecting you, the woman I love. I will never forgive myself for that."

"But you must, Gavin." Diana ran her fingers through his hair, sending a shiver down his spine. "You must forgive yourself, because I already have. I did a long time ago. The question is . . . do you forgive me?"

"Darling, there is nothing to forgive."

They rose at the same time, he from the floor, she from the chair. In two steps she was in his arms, her mouth clinging to his in a desperate kiss filled with love and longing. When they finally pulled apart, Diana leaned her head against his chest.

"My mother told me to listen to my heart," she said, rubbing her cheek against his linen shirt.

"She did?" He stroked her back, loving how she felt in his arms. "And what does your heart say?"

"I love you," she said directly to his own heart.

"And I love you." He kissed the top of her golden head, then looked down at her. "I guess there is only one thing left for me to say." At her questioning look, he asked, "Diana, will you marry me?" When her eyes welled with tears, he said, "Blast, I did it again."

"What?" she asked, wiping her eyes with the back of her free hand.

"Made you cry."

"I always cry when I am happy," she said, touching his face. "I thought you figured that out by now."

"Then I take it your answer is yes?" He held his breath as he waited for her to answer.

She leaned over and kissed him full on the lips. "Yes, my love. I will marry you."

He smiled and gazed into her eyes, unable to get

enough of her. "You have made me the happiest man alive," he said, fingering a strand of her hair. As he continued to drink her in, a sense of peace stole over him. They had both been through so much—the loss of his memory, the death of her husband, the treachery of his cousin. They had escaped their past, but neither of them were unscathed. But they would heal, together. And as soon as he could manage it, this wonderful woman would be his wife, something he had only thought about in his wildest dreams.

"Pinch me," he said suddenly.

She gave him an odd look. "Why?"

"To make sure I am not dreaming."

Instead of a pinch, she gave him a kiss. "Gavin, darling, you are definitely *not* dreaming."

Epilogue

Five years later.

"Papa, swing me around!"

Gavin grabbed his four-year-old daughter around the waist and lifted her high in the air. Violet screeched with delight, her blue eyes, so like her mother's, wide with joy. Hugging her to his chest, his kissed her soft, plump cheek. "I love you, poppet," he said in her ear.

"And I love you, Papa."

He placed her on the ground and gave her a pat on the rump. "Now go find your cousins. They were looking for you earlier."

Violet ran off on chubby legs in search of her eight-year-old cousin Michael, his younger brother, Thomas, and Clarissa, who at age thirteen was the designated nanny of the group. An assignation she adored, as it allowed her to boss the little ones around as long as her heart desired.

He surveyed the surrounding landscape, satisfaction deep within his soul. For the third year in a row the entire Dymoke clan was spending their holiday together at Colin's country house in Leeds. Diana, Colin, and Emily had spent many childhood summers here, and they were passing on the tradition to their own children.

He spied Colin and his wife, Lily, sitting underneath a tree near the house. Colin leaned forward and gave her a passionate kiss, oblivious of who might be watching. Gavin grinned. After nearly fifteen years together, they still acted like newlyweds.

Turning around at the sound of horses approaching, he saw Emily and Michael head for the stables, the sound of their good-natured bickering reaching his ears. Theirs was a lively marriage, and always would be.

He felt the slim arms of his wife encircle his waist. Grasping her hands, he turned her in his arms, then leaned down and kissed her thoroughly.

"Now that is what I call a greeting," she said when he ended the kiss.

"I aim to please."

"You do, darling, you always do."

"Where is your mother?" Gavin asked, not having seen Elizabeth since breakfast.

"Taking a walk with Seamus. You know how they are." Diana feigned disapproval. "Mother said she needs some air, which I find to be an unlikely story. She has never taken to the outdoors like she has since marrying Seamus."

"Seems like my father-in-law has given her a new-found interest in nature."

"Hmph. I believe they are both interested in something, and nature is *not* it."

Gavin laughed. How much he loved his wife and her wicked sense of humor. He kissed the tip of her nose, then moved to her side, wrapping his arm around her slim shoulders. "I love it here," he said.

"I do too. The children adore it as well." She looked up at him coyly. "Speaking of children . . ."

"What?" he said, glancing down at her. When he caught the glow on her face, he gathered her in his arms again. "When did you know?"

"I confirmed it a few days ago." She smiled. "Are you ready for another baby?"

"Are you joking? I am ready for a dozen children." He chuckled as her grin faded. "But only if you want to," he promptly added.

"Let us just work on one at a time."

"I have no objections to that," he quipped. Then he became serious. "When should we tell everyone?"

"Not for a while. I want this to be just between us for a while. Our own little secret."

He hugged her tightly and whispered in her ear. "Have I told you I loved you today?"

"Yes, only a dozen or so times." Then she added against his ear, "But tell me again."